**Danger, Donna Byrd,** *said a little voice in her head.* **Danger!**

But she was in a rather reckless mood. "How interesting would you like to make this?"

He jerked his chin toward the board and, damn, it was sexy.

"If I hit the center," he said, "you will answer any question I ask."

"That's begging for trouble."

"I'll take it easy on you. Promise."

He hit the bull's-eye with no problem.

"Okay. Have at it."

Her choice of words could've been better. Or maybe they were perfect, because a wicked gleam in his gaze told her that she'd hit her own bull's-eye in him.

Caleb sauntered over to the board, plucking out the darts, then leaning against the wall. In his faded blue jeans, tattered boots, long-sleeved white shirt and that hat, he seemed as though he should be out riding the range, not taking aim at her.

But when he did, his aim was true.

"What's the one thing I can do to persuade you to give me a chance, Donna Byrd?"

Dear Reader,

It's been a long stretch of time between the conception of this miniseries to its publication. You see, Judy Duarte, Sheri WhiteFeather and I are critique partners, and we've always wanted to work on a project together—and here it finally is. So this is a very special set of books for us!

In *Tammy and the Doctor,* Judy told the adorable story of the ultimate cowgirl Tammy and how Doc Sanchez fell for her. In *The Texan's Future Bride,* Sheri romanced us with Jenna and J.D., who had lost his memory. Now, in this finale, you'll see how city girl Donna and the charming cowboy Caleb find their way together. (I always did love opposites-attract stories.)

I invite you to come by my website at www.crystal-green.com so you can enter the ongoing contests. You can also follow me on Twitter at @CrystalGreenMe.

All the best,

Crystal Green

# MADE IN TEXAS!

*CRYSTAL GREEN*

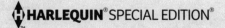
HARLEQUIN® SPECIAL EDITION®

Recycling programs
for this product may
not exist in your area.

ISBN-13: 978-0-373-65741-4

MADE IN TEXAS!

Printed in U.S.A.

## Chapter One

"Whoa there, Lady Bird, let me give you a hand with that."

As Donna Byrd heard the deep, drawling voice behind her, she kept on lifting the hand-carved rocking chair that she'd barely been able to liberate from the bed of one of the Flying B's pickups.

But just as she got the furniture under control, she looked over her shoulder to see who was calling her such a name as "Lady Bird," and her grip faltered.

*Dimples.*

That was what she saw first. Then the light blue eyes that pierced her with an unexpected shock. A shock that she hadn't felt for... Well, a long, long time.

A shock that she really didn't have time for with everything that was going down at the Flying B Ranch.

The owner of those dimples didn't seem to care about Donna's bottlenecked schedules or Byrd family scandals as he grabbed the wobbling rocking chair from her and deftly swung it on to one of his broad shoulders. Then he flashed that smile at her again, his cowboy hat now shading his face from the early July sun. "Where do you need me to put this...?"

"You can call me Donna Byrd," she said, correcting him before he could get too cute and call her Lady Bird again. She gestured toward the main house, with two separate wings spreading out from its core and a wraparound porch. It was the very definition of *Texas cattleman's domain* to her. "You can set the rocker in the living room, if you don't mind."

"I don't mind a bit."

He gave her a long look that covered her all the way from head to toe and sizzled along every inch of skin.

By the time his gaze burned a trail back up her body again, Donna's breath had completely stopped.

Even though she was trying to tell herself that she didn't know him from Adam, she vaguely remembered him. She'd seen him one time, a few months ago, back when her cousin Tammy had injured herself and this same ranch hand had been there to help her out.

He hadn't smiled at her this way, though... At least, Donna didn't think so. She'd been too focused on Tammy's injury to remember. Plus, there'd been a million other things distracting her, like turning the main house and surrounding cabins into a bed-and-breakfast business. She, her sister, Jenna and Tammy had inherited the property from a grandfather none of them had ever met before. Besides that, there were all the personal issues that she'd been trying to deal with.

Even if she had noticed this guy's dimples, she wouldn't have had time for more than a passing glance.

Now he winked at her and carried the rocker up the steps and through the front door she'd already opened. She took a moment, getting her first official good look at him, his worn Wranglers cupping his rear end, his white T-shirt clinging to the muscled lines of his back.

That shock she'd felt before returned with a blast of heat, and she chased it away by shutting the pickup's tailgate, the slam like a punch of reality.

She was thirty-one, too old and too wise to be ogling cowboys. Besides, after she, Jenna and Tammy finished up with all the logistics of the B and B, there would be a big marketing push for Donna to carry out—a task that she had embraced wholeheartedly, since she could accomplish it from New York, where she planned to rent a less costly apartment than she'd had before her grandfather's impending death had summoned all of the Byrd family to Texas. And when she got back to the city, she could return to real life—taking up where she'd left off after her online magazine, *Roxey,* had collapsed. She had ideas for a relaunch under a different title and premise in this new economy....

As she went into the main house, she tried not to think about how the stock market had taken a hit, and how her finances had made her magazine tank. Her wonderful life, her stylish apartment on Manhattan's Upper West Side and nights spent prowling all the new, hot restaurants nearby—it'd all fallen out from under her until Tex Byrd had called.

She silently thanked her grandfather for thinking of his grandkids during his last days. He'd at least been successful in introducing all of them to each other, even if his big hope of reuniting his estranged sons hadn't come true just yet.

In the living room, she found the cheeky ranch hand standing over the rocking chair, which he'd set near a stone fireplace. It was right where she'd been thinking of putting it.

"I appreciate your help," she said, thinking this would be the end of him and she could get back to work.

Yet, he wasn't leaving. No, he was running a hand over the mahogany wood of the high-backed Victorian rocker, making her wonder what it would feel like to have his long fingers mapping *her* with such slow deliberation.

"Where'd you find this beauty?" he asked with that lazy drawl.

She cleared her throat...and her head. "It was in the last abandoned cabin on the property."

"I hear that you and the other Byrd girls have turned all the rest of those cabins upside down and inside out," he said, looking up at her with a grin. "Then you fancied them up with gift baskets and flowers in vases, just like a hotel."

"We want people to be comfortable when they stay here."

God, those dimples. They made her angry for causing such a stir in her. Made her entire body tingle, too.

"It's true," she said, ready to go on her way now. "We Byrd girls have been very hard at work."

"I haven't been back on the Flying B for long, but I've noticed some of the changes you've made to the main house, too—the new swing on the porch outside, the flower garden and fountain you put out back for the guests."

He stood, but he kept a hand on the rocker, his thumb brushing over the carvings of ducks and swans that some man must've painstakingly etched for a woman who'd rocked his child to sleep years and years ago. A strange ache in the center of Donna's chest weighed her down for some reason.

But that was strange, because she'd never planned for children.

No time. Not her, the woman always on the go.

Yet that ache stayed in Donna as she ripped her gaze from the rocking chair and crossed her arms over her chest.

The ranch hand wasn't going anywhere. What—was he expecting a tip, like a doorman?

He sauntered across the room, his boots thudding on the Navajo rug until he got close enough to extend his hand to her.

"It's my turn to introduce myself," he said. "Caleb Granger."

Even his name sounded so very cowboy. Politely, she took his hand and shook it.

"Thank you for your help, Caleb," she said.

Most normal people would've let go of her by now, but not this guy. He kept a hold of her for an extra second—enough to send a pulse of pure need through her fingers and straight down to…

Well, to a location that twisted her around inside.

She let go of him and stepped aside, making it clear that the room's exit was all his.

"So what other gems did you dig up in those old cabins?" he asked, as if he had all the livelong day to charm her.

All right. Maybe it would be a good idea to go along with this. Donna knew full well that she came off as prickly to a lot of people, and she'd been trying to remedy that lately. Honestly, her remoteness was something she'd been aware of for a while now, ever since it had emerged after her parents had divorced and her mom had passed on from cancer when she was nine and Jenna was eight.

People left you. Donna had learned that early in life, and she'd only been readying herself for it to happen again and again.

"We've pulled out some good furniture from the cabins," she said, continuing the small talk. "Cherrywood end tables, a couple of handcrafted cedar chests, cute knickknacks that we've polished up and used to decorate all the guest rooms, even in the main house."

"You're using themes—like the Ace High Saloon Room and Fandango Room."

"We might as well capitalize on the Old West atmosphere of the area. Buckshot Hills has some colorful history to work with."

Donna didn't add that the Flying B had a lot of its own history that wouldn't make it into any room. When she, Jenna and Tammy had gone through what they'd started calling the "dream cabin," they had decided to make only mild improvements to it—especially with the so-called "magical" feather bed stored in there.

Too many weird vibes. Too *much* history for the Byrds.

Family legend had it that when someone slept on that bed, their dreams would come true. Donna hadn't believed a word until Tammy had experienced it firsthand, which had led to her engagement to "Doc" Mike Sanchez, who'd also had a dream. Then the same thing had happened to Jenna and her fiancé, J.D., bringing them together, too.

Yes, Donna was staying as far away from that mattress as possible, because Savannah Jeffries, the woman who'd started all the trouble between Donna's father, Sam, and his twin brother, William, had once slept on that bed, and Donna still wasn't sure what to make of the woman who'd caused all the warring in this family.

The silence between her and this Caleb guy had stretched on for too long, and for the first time, he seemed to be aware of her notorious standoffishness. It'd just taken him a little longer than others to realize it.

"Well then," he said, "if you need any help hauling around more rocking chairs, just give me a holler."

"Okay." Thank goodness, he was finally going to give her some peace.

He tipped his hat to her, and for a moment, she let herself be enthralled with those dimples.

Just one little second.

Then he left the living room, allowing Donna to catch her breath again, once she heard the front door close.

On a whim, she furtively glanced around the room, and since she was quite alone, she wandered over to the window. She peeked around the lace curtains to see Caleb Granger taking his sweet, slow time down the steps, one hand at his waist, his thumb hooked in a belt loop.

She watched until he rounded the corner of the house, no doubt heading toward his side of the ranch, leaving Donna to *her* side.

It took her a minute to recognize that her heart was throbbing—in her neck, in her chest....

And down lower.

But Caleb Granger? Was absolutely *not* her type.

So why was her body trying to tell her differently?

She liked men in pressed suits. Men with some city polish who figuratively got their hands dirty behind a desk, not literally in the stables. Men who smelled like cologne, not...

Saddle soap. Musk.

That was what Caleb Granger had smelled like, come to think of it. And, when Donna had initially come to the Flying B, she'd discovered that being too close to hay made her sneeze, and she'd stayed well away from it ever since, stocking up on allergy medicine and lingering near the main house and cabins instead of the stables.

There was no doubt in her mind that she would be allergic to cowboys like Caleb Granger, too, and that suited her just fine.

Donna was still gazing out the window when she heard a chuckle behind her. Two chuckles.

She looked over her shoulder, to where her cousin and sister stood near the living room entrance. Tammy's dark hair spilled over her shoulders, covering the spaghetti straps of her stylish flowered summer top—one result of a complete makeover for the former tomboy, who could still rope and wrangle with the best of the ranch hands. Jenna, who was the same shade of blond as Donna— although her sister's hair was longer and wavier—was just as pretty in a light blue blouse that brought out the color of her eyes, plus skinny jeans and fashionable yet practical boots.

"What's so funny?" Donna asked.

"You." Jenna leaned against the wall. "We saw you giving him the eye."

Tammy bit down on another laugh.

"Him?" Donna pointed toward the window. "That ranch worker?"

"His name's Caleb Granger," Jenna said.

"Don't I know it." Donna shook her head and walked away from the window, as if to show that she hadn't been interested for even a hot moment. "He made it a major point to introduce himself."

"I think he has a thing for you, Donna." Jenna again.

"He does not."

Tammy spoke up. "The first time he laid eyes on you, he was smitten. And I know the meaning of smitten, since I felt the same way when I met Mike."

A flutter winged around Donna's chest, and she rolled her eyes, thinking that would stop it.

It didn't.

"As if you'd know what Caleb was doing the first time he saw me, Tammy," Donna said. "He was there when you fell and ate it in the dream cabin that day, and you were no doubt hurting too much to dwell on what he was thinking about me. He just didn't leave an impression on *me* because all I cared about was getting you some medical help."

Tammy and Jenna laughed again, and Donna inwardly cringed. They had to be thinking about how clueless she was sometimes, how mired she tended to get in the bigger picture, whether it was Tammy's injury or all the projects they had going on the Flying B. But that's how it had always been with her, because work shut everything else out.

Divorce, death… Work was far more comfortable. And so were goals, like having her own successful magazine and a bright-lights-big-city life again.

Of course, goals could change. Before she'd come to the ranch, she'd never thought about forging a better relationship with the sister she'd been so distanced from her whole life, seeing as Jenna didn't seem to have much in common with Donna when they were young and their dad had raised them to be single-minded women who went after what they wanted, no matter the cost. She'd never thought about getting close to the cousins she'd never known, either.

But losing Grandpa Tex just when he'd come into her life had shown Donna, once again, that you had to tread lightly with others, that getting close was still a chancy proposition that she was just now dipping her toes into.

Not too deeply, though.

Never too deeply.

After Tammy and Jenna had laughed it up quite thoroughly, Tammy said, "I hear that most girls do remember Caleb. *Really* well."

Jenna added, "*I* hear there're more than a few of them, too."

"Who knows how many there've been since he's been off the Flying B?" Tammy gave Donna a sly glance. "He took a leave of absence for some family matters—something about helping his father and aunt move to Buckshot Hills and get settled."

"J.D. took his job in the stables for a while," Jenna said.

At least Donna had been paying enough attention to know that Jenna had met J.D. when he'd been wandering the Flying B Road to the ranch. He had lost his memory, and Jenna had helped nurse him back to health along with Doc, until J.D. had regained his senses.

Jenna was waggling her eyebrows. "But now Caleb's back—and this time it looks like Donna actually had time to notice."

Tammy cracked up again as Donna sighed in exasperation. Maybe she *had* noticed, but it didn't matter. Not when she had a million things to do today.

And definitely not when she wasn't planning to stay around the Flying B for much longer, anyway.

After leaving the main house, it hadn't taken Caleb long to hitch a ride at the barn with old Hugh in his Dodge.

They rambled along on the dirt road leading out to the east boundary of the ranch, where they were going to mend fences today. Before they'd hopped into the truck, Hugh, the foreman, had introduced Caleb to J.D., the man who'd taken Caleb's place during his leave of absence.

"He's been a real find," Hugh said now, "but we missed you, boy. Nothing's been the same without you around."

"Same here, boss."

Caleb rested his bare forearm on the windowsill as the truck grumbled along, passing the fields that yawned under a sky that reminded him of Donna Byrd's eyes. He'd been thinking about her since the day he'd met her. Or *not* met her, to be more exact. She'd been a little... *distracted* might be a good word, but, then again, it'd been a trying day for the Byrds after Tammy's tumble and fall, then her visit to the doctor. So how could he blame Donna for being preoccupied?

Still, Caleb was used to making more of an impression on women, and Donna's cool attitude puzzled him. It also lit a fire in him that he'd never felt before, because good times had always come so easy.

And that was something Donna Byrd was obviously not. Easy.

She was sophisticated, dignified and more beautiful than anyone he'd ever set eyes on. There was something else about her, though, that got to Caleb. A depth. A sort of sadness that he'd caught a few months ago as well as today, and she only seemed to show it when she thought no one was looking, covering it up before a person could be sure.

Yet that was another challenge about Donna Byrd— seeing if he could make that hint of darkness go away.

And, Lord knew, Caleb knew about a little darkness.

"I missed the Flying B more than you know," Caleb said.

"You didn't exactly take a vacation."

"Right." Caleb turned to Hugh. "Have you ever spent any amount of time off the ranch? You never seem to take a break from it."

"No reason to." The old man pursed his lips. "I grew up here, just like you, and this is where I prefer to be above anywhere else."

"Then you'd have the same reaction to the suburbs as I did. Buckshot Hills is still country, but some of it's developing. I moved my dad and Aunt Rosemary into a new place—Yellow Rose Estates, they call it."

"Sounds uppity."

"It's modest. A bunch of tract houses that all look the same. But it's safe and close enough for me to visit when I need to."

They hit a rut in the road, and the truck creaked on its springs.

"How is the old man doing?" Hugh asked.

Caleb shrugged, and that was enough of an answer. Some days with his dad's worsening dementia were good, some weren't so much. Mostly they weren't, though, and Caleb had endured a lot of those days this past month or so, as he'd finalized the purchase of a new home for Aunt Rosemary and his dad and moved them from her former house near Dallas.

He could just see his aunt now, as they set up his dad's room with his sleep apnea equipment and the walker he refused to use as much as he should.

"We're so grateful for everything you're doing, Caleb." Rosemary had seemed so tiny, sitting on the bed in a pair of sweats, her hair gray and thinner than it had ever been. But she had smiled as she talked, her cheeks soft and rosy, as she'd glanced around her new home.

Ten years older than Dad, Rosemary had always been a maternal figure for him since they'd lost their parents early on, sticking with each other through thick and thin. She'd insisted on taking care of him now, too, especially since Dad's dander rose whenever Caleb was around.

Yup, Caleb knew that Aunt Rosemary was grateful. Not so much Dad, though.

"It's the least I can do," he'd said to her.

They hadn't talked about how he and his dad hadn't ever been good buddies or how he had always refused any of Caleb's help, even back when he'd been in his right mind. An only child, Caleb had been too much of a "party boy," in Dad's estimation; although, as Caleb had matured, he'd always lived up to every vow he'd made and every responsibility he'd had. But that had happened only after Mom had died, shortly after Caleb had graduated from the local high school and he'd left home, finding work at the Flying B, where he'd pretty much been raised the rest of the way to adulthood by Tex Byrd and the ranch hands.

It seemed as if Hugh had sensed the direction of Caleb's thoughts.

"You know you've got family here, Caleb. You always have and you always will. You were like Tex's own son."

Tex. Even the sound of his name made Caleb's chest hurt.

"Hey," Hugh said. "I know what you're thinkin', and it isn't right."

"What?"

"That you weren't around when Tex passed on. It wasn't your fault that he lied to you about just how sick the doc said he was when he told you to go on and see to your own dad's needs. He would've been fit to be tied if you'd stayed with him and refused to see to your father."

That much was true. Tex had been adamant about Caleb making up with Dad, no doubt because the family rift with the Byrds had gone on for so long and Tex regretted that he'd missed out on being a part of his own children's—and grandchildren's—lives.

The last thing Caleb had wanted was for Tex to be disappointed in him, so he'd gone. But he hadn't made it back to the Flying B in time—he'd only been here for the funeral, staying in the background before seeing to the last of Dad and Aunt Rosemary's new home—and that dogged him.

Grieving for Tex alone. Wishing he could've done something to keep him around for much, much longer.

Even with the note Tex had left him, telling him how proud he was of Caleb and how he hadn't wanted Caleb to see him wasting away in his final days, there was still that raw sense of loss and failure.

Hugh gave him another sidelong look, and Caleb decided to move on.

"The Flying B's a different place without him, isn't it?"

"It's a kind of different that Tex would've approved of. When he gave the girls the east side of the property, with the ranch and its buildings, and the Byrd boys the land that wasn't being used, he stipulated that they use their inheritance money to develop both sides after he passed away."

"I like what they're doing."

"I hear you like even more than that."

Caleb grinned. "It's no secret I get along with women."

Hugh's chuckle was a rasp. "The snooty Byrd isn't the one I would've chosen for you."

"Donna Byrd isn't snooty. She's just a fish out of water."

"And you'll reel her in. Is that right?"

"Why not? It's about time I settled down."

He'd come to that conclusion after seeing Donna for the first time. It'd been an instant, overwhelming attraction, even if it would be a challenge to hook her.

Hugh shook his head, and it rankled Caleb. Maybe the older ranch hand thought Donna was out of Caleb's league, or that a ladies' man like him would never settle down for anyone, even a Byrd. Or maybe Hugh was even thinking that Donna might be way too much trouble for him in the long run and he shouldn't pin his hopes on anything with her.

But Caleb couldn't blame his friend for any of that. No one, not even Hugh, knew how much of a father figure Tex had become to Caleb after he'd taken him in— even more than his own dad. Tex had sorely missed his own sons, and somehow, Caleb had filled a void, sitting down with him on the main house's old creaky porch swing after a long day, smoking cigars, talking for hours and drinking the good bourbon and wine Tex used to collect. The old man had never told Caleb the details about what had torn apart his relationship with his sons Sam and William—and what had made them dislike each other so intensely that it'd caused a tear that made their relationship ragged even today. But Caleb had heard rumors around the ranch, anyway, about how Savannah Jeffries had been dating one twin, William, during college. She'd come home with him one summer, after he'd suffered a broken leg in a car accident, and during his convalescence, she'd supposedly fallen for Sam, Donna's father.

Nope, no one knew just how much Tex had meant to Caleb.

Hugh sighed gruffly as he pulled the truck off the road, toward the fences that required their labors.

He turned off the engine. "Maybe you think that there's some kind of love bug going around since the Byrd kids have come back, Caleb, but from what I hear, Donna's probably immune to it. She's a cool one."

"I've melted my share," Caleb said.

"So you have." Hugh grabbed Caleb's shirtsleeve before he could open the door. "Just keep in mind that she's got a lot going on."

Although the older man didn't explain further, Caleb knew that Hugh only meant to protect him, and he gave the man a gentle, fond shove.

"Don't worry about me, boss." He exited the truck, his boots hitting the dirt.

He was as grounded as ever, with his feet back on familiar territory.

And he was just as determined to show Donna Byrd that he was more than merely a heart-struck cowboy.

## Chapter Two

At the first peek of dawn, Donna was up and about because, no matter how long she'd been in Texas, she was still on New York time—an hour ahead of the dear Old West.

After doing a quick check of her email—nothing new or exciting there—she tucked her iPad into the crook of her arm, then went to the kitchen to grab one of the luscious chocolate chip muffins Barbara the cook had already made. After downing that, then a mug of Earl Grey tea, she scooted out the back door before a real breakfast could be served buffet style in the dining room.

A million things to do, Donna thought as she made her way to the nearest renovated cabin. And the first item on her list was to double—no, *quadruple*—check this particular room's condition.

It had cute embroidered curtains and valances, rustic Southwestern furniture, faux-Remington sculptures and "hotel amenities," as Caleb Granger might've called the fancy bathroom vanity basket that included everything from soaps and shampoos to more private items, like toothbrushes and even condoms for the younger, hip crowd they were targeting for business. But, at the sight of that last item, a flurry of sensation attacked Donna, and she frowned, turning away from the bathroom sink and its basket.

Putting Caleb Granger and condoms in the same train of thought brought back those tingles she'd been trying to ignore ever since she'd officially met him yesterday.

Yet she left all of that behind as she focused—and focused *hard,* to tell the truth—on switching a rugged cowboy sculpture on one oak end table with a second horse sculpture on a highboy chest by the door.

Afterward, she stood back to assess the look of the room again.

Not bad. Not bad at all. The Flying B and B would impress anyone, even the college friend she'd invited for the weekend. Theo Blackwood worked at *Western Horizons* travel magazine, and Donna hoped he would be swayed enough by the ranch to do a layout during their grand opening in a little less than a couple of months.

After brushing some dust off the rough cowboy sculpture, Donna couldn't find anything else to nitpick. It all really was tip-top. That's how everything *needed* to be. That's how life had always been for her, and someday soon, it would be that way again. All she needed to do was create a smashing success of this B and B, and she would be on her way out of Hoop-De-Do, Texas, and back to the glamour and rush-rush of the big city.

She sat on the bed, the foam mattress and beige duvet as comfortable as sin, then fired up her iPad. The screen

saver still featured the swirly, creamy logo she'd com-
missioned for *Roxey* magazine, but instead of feeling
sorrow at its demise, Donna only wanted to live up to
its failed promise.

But first, there were personal matters to attend to.
One of her To-Do's today was an activity she managed
*every* day—tapping the name Savannah Jeffries into an
internet search engine. She was hoping that this time of
all times she would discover something new that their
P.I., Roland Walker, hadn't found out about the woman
who'd torn this family apart.

Yet all that popped up on the screen were the same
old results and links Donna always got, so she checked
her email for the second time this morning.

But there was no word from their P.I., either, even
though Donna contacted him religiously.

She blew out a breath. She didn't like being ruled by
anything—another person, life's circumstances…even
a growing obsession like this one. And just why *did* Savannah have a hold on her? Maybe it was because Donna
had taken such stock in whatever her father, Sam, had
taught her throughout life—at least, before he'd fallen
from grace in Donna's and Jenna's eyes.

*Know your opponents,* he would say from behind his
corporate desk whenever he brought her and Jenna to
work. *Don't ever let them surprise you*.

But was Savannah the enemy? Or was it her dad, who
had betrayed Uncle William and stolen his own brother's girlfriend that one summer when they'd all been on
the Flying B?

She kept remembering something else her dad had
taught her and Jenna. *Go after what you want at any
cost, girls…*

His voice faded from Donna, and she tried to believe it didn't matter. Ever since the news about Savannah had come out, she'd been avoiding Dad. It'd been easy, too, since he was off with Uncle William again, this time in Hill Country, hunting and trying to iron everything out with his twin.

She was still attempting to figure out how she could talk to the stranger that Dad had become. They'd never been ultraclose, but she'd worshipped him as a daughter; she'd at least *thought* she'd known who he was, and it wasn't a man who would work his brother over.

Chasing all the alienating numbness away, Donna fully immersed herself in her computer, mostly with news of the publishing world. She liked the isolation of the cabin since it allowed her to get a lot of work done without interruption.

Then she heard something outside the door.

Boot steps on the small porch.

A knock.

Finally, the whisper of the door as it opened to let in a stream of morning sunlight.

"Anyone home?" asked a voice that had become all too familiar to Donna, since she couldn't seem to forget what it had sounded like yesterday when it had scratched down her skin, infiltrating her every vibrating cell.

Caleb Granger.

She sat up straight on the bed. "I'm in here."

Dumbest announcement ever, but what else could she do? Pretend she was invisible, just so he would go away?

When he pushed open the door, her heart started to beat with such an all-consuming volume that she could barely hear herself breathing.

Or maybe, just like yesterday, she'd stopped breathing

altogether at the sight of Caleb Granger in those boots, Wranglers and T-shirt.

And when he doffed his cowboy hat in her presence to reveal shaggy dark blond hair, then smiled with those lethal dimples, she wasn't sure she would ever breathe again.

The mere sight of the early light flirting with Donna Byrd's shoulder-length blond hair and her skin, which she somehow kept smooth and creamy out here in the elements, was enough to send Caleb's pulse into a kicking frenzy.

She was something to behold, sitting on a bed wearing a sleeveless white halter top that was kind to every curve of her body. Her creased dark blue shorts clung to her lush hips, and even her Keds somehow came off as classy. She was certainly a far cry from when he'd seen her that first day, months ago, in suede boots and an expensive outfit that had marked her as anything but a country girl.

She seemed to realize that she was sitting on a bed, and she stood, brushing off her shorts with one hand while the other put one of those computer pad things that everyone in the suburbs had seemed so enthralled with down on the mattress. He noticed a fancy logo on the screen saver and recalled some gossip about a defunct magazine she'd run back in the city.

Drive and gumption. That's what this woman had, and hard times hadn't seemed to dampen her ambition at all, based on what she was doing with the B and B.

"Can I do something for you?" she asked.

He wasn't going to touch that innuendo-rife question

with a ten-foot stick. "I saw you headed in here earlier, and I thought I'd say a good morning."

For the first time in Caleb's life, a woman was looking at him as if she couldn't understand why in the world he would've gone out of his way for something so unimportant.

Was Hugh right when he'd told Caleb yesterday that Donna Byrd wasn't winnable? Or was she so far into her own business that she had no idea that Caleb was even interested?

Well, he didn't know just what to think of either option, but it didn't stop him from making himself at home and leaning against the door frame.

"I suppose I had another reason for stopping in," he said, flashing his smile at her again, pulling out the big guns.

She wrinkled her brow, as if he were a creature who'd wandered out from the woods, a previously unidentified species that absolutely perplexed her.

"Your reason being…?" she asked.

"Simple hospitality."

She laughed. "I've gotten plenty of that, Mr. Granger. Everyone on the Flying B has been more than cordial."

"And I'll extend that trend by asking you to call me Caleb. There's no need for 'misters' around here."

"Caleb it is, then."

Now she was looking at him expectantly. But that—and the compelling depth of her blue eyes—only made him forge on.

He'd never turned down a challenge before, and now wouldn't be the first time.

"Word has it that you're putting on some sort of movie night this weekend," he said.

"Oh. Right. Yes, we're attaching a screen to the side of the barn and setting up a picnic area in front of it for the staff, just like we'll be doing for our guests when we open the B and B. Barbara is planning a country menu, so you could call this a dry run for the real thing."

"A *country* menu? You mean basic Texas staples, like barbecue baby back ribs and steaks, hot biscuits and corn?"

"That's exactly what I meant." She stuffed her hands into her pockets. "We've got a special guest coming to the Flying B this weekend, so that's another reason for the show. He's a journalist friend of mine, and we're hoping he'll write an article for a B and B marketing push."

All Caleb heard was "friend" and "he."

"A friend, huh?" he asked carelessly.

"Yes, a…" She narrowed her eyes at him. "Never mind."

"No, go on, Lady Bird. I'm just curious."

"First off, my name's not Lady Bird."

Caleb smiled. "Okay, Donna Byrd." He liked the ring of that better, anyway. The way it flowed made her sound exotic, which she was to him; it made her sound as if she was a hothouse breed. But even if she wasn't so *hothouse* on the surface, Caleb would bet there was a soft, melting center to her, and he was going to find it.

She didn't seem amused by the adjustment to the nickname. "You were about to tell me why you were here?"

Yeah, that. "As I said—movie night. There's a lot of excitement in the air. Everyone's talking about how the ranch hasn't seen much in the way of celebration since Tex passed on."

He hadn't meant to change tone after saying Tex's name. Quieter. Reflecting a grief that still lingered.

When Donna removed her hands from her pockets and slightly tilted her head, as if in sympathy, he stood away from the door frame.

He hadn't come here to be a downer.

"I heard that you were close to Tex," she said softly. "I barely got to know him, but..."

She pressed her lips together, as if banning herself from saying anything else.

Yet he'd seen that sorrow in her gaze, and as much as she was attempting to cover it now, it wasn't working.

She cleared her throat. "I'm sorry for your loss."

"And yours," Caleb said.

She paused, then casually walked to the other side of the bed, straightening the thick quiltlike thing on top of it, but her actions didn't fool him for a moment. She was putting a barrier between them, just as she did with everyone else.

Good try.

"As far as movie night goes," he said, getting back on the subject, "I was only wondering what your plans were for it."

Donna stopped her fussing with the bed and watched him again, obviously trying to sort out his true meaning.

Caleb put on the charm once more. "I thought I'd bring some wine and—"

"Are you inviting me to my own function?"

"In a manner of speaking, yes, I am." He shrugged. "You'll have to take a break sometime that night."

Astonishment. Was that what he was seeing on her now?

He'd take it, because that meant he was getting a rise

out of her, and if there was nothing about her that was interested in *him,* she wouldn't have bothered with any kind of reaction.

"You've got some chutzpah," she finally said.

"What I've also got is great taste in wine."

"Do you really."

"Sure. Tex and I used to sit on his porch swing and talk about everything while we drank from his spirits collection. He was a wine guy, you know."

Donna had her arms crossed over her chest now. She seemed to do that around Caleb frequently.

"I saw his cellar," she said. "It *is* extensive."

"He had vintages shipped from all over—Napa Valley, Bordeaux, Chile, the Rioja region of Spain."

She surveyed him, seemingly taking a second look at the cowboy loitering near the doorway, and hope sprang in Caleb's chest.

Was she seeing beyond the Stetson and boots?

When she went back to straightening the pillows on the bed, he wasn't so sure.

"Thanks for the offer for movie night," she said, "but I'm afraid I won't have a second to rest."

Caleb let her excuse go. If she didn't come around this weekend, he would find another time to be alone with Donna Byrd.

Before he went, he took one last opportunity to be complimentary, glancing around the room. "As I said yesterday, you've done a real good job with the ranch so far. You should be proud."

She actually beamed, and it made him think that all the trouble she'd been dealing to him had been worth it.

"That's nice of you to say," she said.

"It's just the truth."

She sat on the bed, as if forgetting he was in the room and she had been using the mattress as an obstacle only a short time before.

Beds.

Donna Byrd.

*Stop it, Caleb.*

She said, "I've been going over the cabins again and again, looking for faults. It's good to hear that we've been successful."

"There's one place that you left out of your makeover, though. Savannah's old cabin."

The name hovered, as if circling them.

But if he was going to get to know Donna Byrd, Savannah was bound to come up sometime or another.

"It's a cabin that's just as good as any of the others," he said.

"No. That antique bed has been stored in there for a while, and… Well, we modernized the kitchen, but moving anything else around in there seems like bad luck or something."

This was unexpected. Was she superstitious?

Maybe she would believe in fate just as much as he did—that his destiny was tied to hers….

"You know all about that bed," she said. "Don't pretend you're oblivious."

"Tex told me a thing or two about it." *But not everything, I suppose.*

"I know that my great-grandmother first brought that bed to the ranch. This sounds like such a cliché, but she was supposed to have the gift of second sight, and she would dream of the future when she slept on that feather mattress." She hesitated, then said, "I know other people who've had…experiences…in the bed, too."

"You?"

It was dangerous to ask such a forthcoming question about beds. About Donna Byrd.

But she didn't shoot him one of those *what-are-you-all-about?* looks this time. She only laughed a little.

"No, I haven't been on the bed. But I do wonder if Savannah ever had dreams there since she stayed in that cabin."

"You think you'll have the chance to ask her?"

Now he knew he'd gone too far, because she stiffened.

Was she thinking that Byrd business was Byrd business, and he had no part of it?

Before he could decide, she gave him a curious look. "You haven't been around the ranch in a while, right?"

Aha, she'd noticed. The news did him good. "Right."

"There's a lot that's been happening with Savannah Jeffries. Nobody caught you up on all of it?"

"I'm afraid not."

Donna sighed. "Tammy found a grocery receipt while she was snooping around Savannah's cabin. You remember that day."

The day Tammy had injured herself in the cabin and he'd first seen Donna. He'd never forget.

"A receipt?" he asked.

"It was from the time Savannah spent on the ranch, and there was a pregnancy test on it."

Caleb froze. "Are you saying there might be another Byrd running around out there?"

"There could be."

He was getting better and better at recognizing Donna's body language. She was already shutting him out with her cool voice. But damned if he'd let her do that. He had an investment in this family, too, an interest in seeing that Tex's love for this land and his family was never tarnished.

But Caleb would have plenty of time for trying to make Donna come around, and he moseyed toward the door. "You'll want to be deciding on your favorite vintage, Donna Byrd. I'll have it ready when you are."

He received one of her miffed expressions in return, putting them back to where they'd been when he'd first entered the cabin. And just before it seemed that she was about to follow it up with a tart remark, the sound of a cell phone—a businesslike digital ring—interrupted them.

She stood, reaching into her pocket to answer as Caleb smiled at her in parting.

As he exited, he glanced back, just one more time, and when he found that Donna Byrd was watching him while answering her phone, he went on his way, his smile growing even wider.

Hours later, Donna was in her room in the main wing of the big house, sitting in the bay window and rubbing her temples to chase away a headache as she waited to go downstairs to share the news from the call she'd received earlier.

She was still reeling from what their investigator, Roland Walker, had told her, and, surprisingly, the only thing that was keeping her from stressing out entirely was the thought of Caleb and his promises of wine.

How strange was it that Caleb seemed to be her only bright spot during the day? She wouldn't have predicted that in a thousand years because he was a distraction. A man with a killer smile who only messed up her head and took her offtrack.

But every time he would cross her thoughts—and he seemed to be doing that quite a bit—she would find herself fighting a smile.

*Her*—the remote Byrd. The prickly one who had never found the kind of love Tammy and Doc or Jenna and J.D. had, and the one who probably never would, based on her record of dating, then deciding her time was better spent on whatever project she had on the front burner.

Speaking of which…

Her alarm clock read 5:00 p.m., and she inhaled, standing, then leaving her bedroom. When she got to the living room, everyone was waiting: Jenna, who sat in the new rocking chair by the fireplace; Tammy, who perched on a leather sofa in between her brothers, Aidan and Nathan, both dwarfing her with their size.

"What's so all-fire important that you pulled me out of my cabin?" Nathan, the younger brother, asked lightly. He and Aidan hadn't just been staying in their own cabins on the property, they had been making improvements bit by bit, practicing their home contracting business skills on the Flying B's structures.

Donna tried to smile at Nathan's high spirits. At least her cousin's jocular sense of humor was intact…for now.

Aidan, the serious one, merely waited for Donna to start.

"I got some good news today from Roland Walker." Donna had learned from Dad that you always started out positive if you were about to lower the boom on someone. "But it's also news you'll want to brace yourselves for."

Jenna sat forward in the rocking chair. "Roland found out that Savannah did have a child?"

Donna nodded, letting them all take that in.

On the sofa, Tammy bit her lip, suppressing a smile. She'd been the most curious out of all of them when it came to Savannah. Jenna just sat back in her chair, thoughtful, but Aidan was running a hand through his black hair, cursing under his breath, exchanging a look with an equally darkened Nathan.

"It's a boy," Donna said, still not knowing exactly how she felt about all of this, herself, now that matters had gone so far. "His name is James Bowie Jeffries."

Aidan let loose with that curse, following up with, "Are you kidding me? That woman had the gall to name him—"

"In the same way our dads were named?" Nathan interrupted, his mood definitely blacker.

"William Travis Byrd," Aidan said. "Sam Houston Byrd. Now James Bowie Jeffries. All named after Texas heroes."

"Except James Bowie isn't a Byrd," Nathan said, all traces of humor gone now.

Tammy said, "*I* have to admire Savannah."

"For what?" both brothers asked.

"For owning what she did." Tammy's black hair swung over her shoulders as she looked at one brother, then the other. "I wonder if she told James who the father was or if she raised him to be a Byrd."

"What *is* a Byrd?" Aidan asked. "None of us even knew that until we met Tex, and based on what we gleaned from the little our dads have told us, Tex didn't want any part of Savannah. So how would *she* know the definition?"

Nathan folded his bulky arms over an equally wide chest. "Tex threw her off this ranch after he found Sam and her together then everyone went their separate ways."

The last thing Donna wanted was for this to disintegrate into a Sam versus William match. All of them were getting along way too well for that to happen.

"The bottom line is," she said, "we're going to have to make a decision. It doesn't have to be tonight, but Roland said he can track James down if we want to meet him."

The boys chuffed.

Jenna rose from the rocking chair. "He's our brother… or cousin. Any way you put it, James is one of us."

Aidan stopped laughing. "That's another thing. I'd like to know just why it is he *needs* to be tracked down. Roland found Savannah already. Why isn't James easier to find?"

Donna automatically walked toward her sister, whom she had supported during the family's first vote, when they had debated whether to hire a P.I. to investigate Savannah in the first place. She'd had mixed feelings about locating Savannah then, too, but she had wanted to turn over a new leaf and support Jenna and her desire to find Savannah more than anything else.

"Roland told me," Donna said, "that James and Savannah are estranged."

"Seems like she has somewhat of a pattern," Aidan muttered.

Tammy elbowed him in the ribs and he gritted his jaw.

"Why're they estranged?" she asked.

Donna shook her head. "Roland doesn't have that information right now, but we could ask him to find out."

Now Nathan was on his feet. "This is how I see it—we've already had any curiosity about Savannah appeased." He shot a look to Tammy, making sure everyone knew that she had been working overtime to assuage his feelings about *that* family decision. "But do we really want to take this further?"

Aidan stood, too, and although Nathan was a big man, his older brother was even larger. "Right now, we don't know who fathered James. I'm fine with keeping it that way."

"Why?" Tammy asked from her seat on the sofa.

"Because knowing the answer is going to put a real wedge between all of us," Aidan said. "Can you imagine trying to work together on the Flying B after we know the truth? Tex didn't bequeath his properties to us in order to tear us apart—he wanted us to stay together."

Nathan raised a finger. "We haven't even talked about what kind of canyon this is going to put between our dads. They're off traipsing around the wilderness right now on some male twin bonding ritual that I hope will finally do the trick and bring them together again, and here we are, debating about ruining that. They both have egos, and…"

Donna had gone pricklier than ever. "You mean my dad has the ego, don't you?"

Jenna came closer to her as the boys, and even Tammy, got an *I'm-not-saying-another-word-about-that* look on their faces.

Donna sighed. "It's true that our dads have mended a lot of old wounds lately. But part of me wonders if putting this information in a proverbial closet will do more damage than ever."

Then again, no one was talking about how James might feel about a decision that was really his.

"I agree about ignoring the truth," Tammy said. "We should just lay everything to rest *now*. It could be that the revelation of whose son James really is will heal us altogether since *not* knowing would eat away at us and make things much worse."

Silence bit the room until Jenna took a breath, then spoke.

"We should get in touch with our dads to see what they think."

When Donna glanced at Jenna, she knew that her sister would take it upon herself to contact their father since she had already reconciled with him. Donna sent her a smile of thanks, even while she ached to talk to him, too.

But how, after everything he'd done to let her down?

Tammy fetched a phone from a holster on her jeans. "I'm calling Dad now. I talked to him last night, so I'll bet they're within service range."

"We really want to ruin their idyllic nature walk?" Nathan asked.

Tammy moved her thumb over her smart phone screen. "I don't see that there's a choice. They can hash this out together in the boonies."

"*My* vote's still a big no about having our P.I. find the kid," Aidan said.

Nathan chuffed. "That 'kid' is just a little bit older than Donna."

This seemed to bug him, too, since it was obvious that his uncle Sam had gone straight into the arms of another woman—Donna and Jenna's mom—after his affair with Savannah. Honestly, Donna didn't like the thought of this, either, because it made it seem as if love was cheap to Dad. She'd never known that about him. Never even expected that he could be so loose with his affections, and it made her feel protective for Mom, even if she'd been gone a long time.

"All the same," Nathan added, "I vote no on this situation, too."

"It's a yes for me," Jenna said, "and I'm guessing Tammy, as well."

As Tammy nodded, she glanced at Donna, and no one had to tell her that she just might be the tiebreaker, depending on what their dads said.

Jenna jerked her chin toward the room's exit, and it was apparent that she wanted a private word with Donna.

As they left the room, Jenna addressed Tammy. "Can you give us a few minutes before you call Uncle William? I'd like to reach Dad at the same time, if possible."

"Sure."

And, while they exited, Tammy launched into every argument she could probably think of to sway her brothers.

After a little walking down the hall, Jenna pulled Donna into the dining room, the dark wood and stag horns above the long table looking more imposing than usual.

Jenna shut the double doors behind her. "You don't seem convinced, Donna."

Was it that obvious? "I'm sorry. But the ramifications of *this* decision could be…"

"A real challenge? We're up to it."

For the first time in Donna's life, she actually felt as if she was close enough to her sister so that she could confide in her. The realization tightened her throat, and she had a hard time getting the words out.

"It's just that we were about to mend all of our own fences because of our dads, and then Tammy found that clue about Savannah's baby. We were doing so well for a while."

"You're still mad at Dad for being with Savannah, aren't you? He didn't try to fall in love with her, Donna."

"He didn't try to stop having sex with his brother's girlfriend, either." Harsh. But this wasn't the man Donna had grown up idolizing.

She calmed down. "I just remember how he used to tell us to go after everything we wanted, Jen. It looks like he really practiced what he preached, and the fall-out isn't pretty."

Jenna laid a hand on Donna's arm. She was getting used to the contact. Donna's *friends* didn't even show this kind of sympathy, but since coming to the Flying B, Donna had begun to wonder if she'd actually had friends or just people she went out with after work at night to blow off steam.

"After I finally talked to Dad about this," Jenna said, "I found out that he was inconsolable when Savannah left the ranch and disappeared afterward. He got hurt in this, too, and I only came to understand that after I fell in love myself."

Was she saying that Donna didn't have a chance in hell of understanding since she had no one?

An image of dimples flashed into her mind. Pale blue eyes sparkling with humor and lightness.

Caleb.

She shook him off. "Yeah, Dad was so inconsolable that he married Mom on the rebound. No wonder they split up."

"Donna, you really should talk to him. We can call, right now."

Her stomach turned with nerves. "No. I don't want to say to him what I have to say over the phone."

"Then when will you do it?"

"Soon." She walked to the doors, paused. "Thanks for taking care of this, though. It means a lot."

Jenna merely nodded as Donna opened the doors, closing them behind her, yet hardly shutting out her sister's voice as she said, "Hey, Dad, it's Jenna."

As Donna walked away, her footsteps echoed off the walls, the sound mocking the dull thud of every isolated heartbeat.

## Chapter Three

Chow time at the ranch employee cabins was never a dull affair.

The next night, while Caleb sat next to Hugh at a long dinner table outside the mess hall, the usual end-of-the-day cowboy talk swarmed around them, just as thick as the smoke coming off the barbecue. On the other side of Caleb, a young ranch hand named Manny plopped down on the bench, immediately pushing back his hat to reveal a patch of curly brown hair before chomping into his corn bread.

"Did y'all hear about the hot times in the main house last night?" he asked with his mouth full, nodding his head toward the Byrds' domain.

Caleb, who'd already pushed away his emptied tin plate, leaned his elbows on the table while holding a beer bottle between two fingers. Donna was in that house, and he was all ears.

Hugh was nursing a ceramic mug of coffee. "There've been more than a few hot times since the Byrd kids came home to roost."

"But last night was a real doozy." Manny dipped his bread into his chili bowl. "Maria and I have both been working, so she told me about it only an hour ago when she took a break."

Caleb glanced at Hugh, who cocked his bushy eyebrow in response. Manny was dating a housemaid, so she must've been dusting or some-such last night while the Byrds conducted business.

"How much of a doozy was it?" Caleb asked, turning back to Manny.

"On a scale of calm to loud, it was at about a bellow. Maria said that the little Byrds were going at it like they were on the *Maury* show, including a lot of who's-the-daddy talk."

Caleb recalled what Donna had told him about Savannah's pregnancy test. "Is there a long-lost kid?"

"Yup, their P.I. located him," Manny said. "And it really chapped some of their hides that Savannah named him in the style of Tex's boys. James Bowie Jeffries is what he's called."

Next to Caleb, Hugh made a grumbling sound, seeming to be just as offended as some of the Byrds apparently were.

Then Hugh said, "Did Maria have her ear to the door or something?"

"Very funny, old-timer." Manny polished off the last of his chili, standing to get seconds, like he always did. "No matter how Maria heard it, she didn't like the news. That family is coming apart at the seams now that Tex is gone, and she doesn't know how long we might have jobs here."

Caleb put down his beer. "That's a load of bull, Manny, and you know it."

"Do I? Caleb, we don't know these Byrd kids from seven holes in the ground. I like them well enough, but what if they end up dismantling the Flying B? What if Tex was all that was keeping the ranch together?"

Something seemed to crack in Caleb, breaking him in a thousand directions inside. This was his home—the only one he'd ever felt comfortable in after his mom had passed on.

Manny had gone back to the food station, leaving Hugh and Caleb alone.

The foreman chucked the rest of his coffee on the ground.

"Before Tex died," Caleb said, "he told me that, under the conditions of his will, the ranch couldn't be dismantled. The grandkids have to spend their inheritance on bettering it, so Manny's worrying for nothing."

"It's not the ranch I'm thinking about." Hugh ran a hand over his grizzled face. "You can't have more than one person inheriting something and expect them to all agree on every decision."

"So you're worried about the family itself. Boss, you've sure become pessimistic about things lately."

"And why shouldn't I be? It might be time to retire, live off my savings, fish all day. Who needs all this nonsense?"

Hugh's words were flippant, but Caleb knew better. Like him, the foreman loved this place, as well as the ragtag family of ranch hands that Tex had put together.

Gathering his plate, Caleb prepared to go.

"Where're you off to?" Hugh asked.

"Where do you think?"

"Aw, no." Hugh shook his finger at Caleb. "You're not going to the house like I think you are."

"I am. There's no way I'm going to see a rift destroy Tex's family."

"So what're you gonna do—help Donna Byrd carry in another rocking chair and chide her about family business at the same time? That's no way to get into her good graces, son."

"This has nothing to do with that. She and the others need to know that we—the staff—have a stake in seeing the family at peace, too."

"You're overstepping, Caleb."

Was he?

Would Tex have told him that, too?

The last time Caleb had seen him, lying in bed, looking like half the hale-and-hearty man he'd always been, Tex had told Caleb that he would be leaving him a bit of money. Not a whole lot, but enough to tell him that he valued him.

"Money doesn't show everything that's in a person's heart, though," Tex had said.

"Of course it doesn't."

He had closed his eyes, so weary. "If I could buy goodwill from my sons and their children, I would. I'd do anything for them to realize that they could have something wonderful out here on the Flying B together. At least you've always known what you've got on this ranch, Caleb."

"That's right, Tex."

The money hadn't been the point, though. In fact, Caleb had never expected to be treated like Tex's blood, and he'd been blown away that the man had even given him some seed money for his own future. Naturally, he'd spent it well, on the new house he'd purchased for his dad and aunt, but it was too bad money couldn't buy a positive word from his father during one of his more lucid times, either.

Now, Caleb began to walk away from the table, saying over his shoulder, "Tex would've wanted me to interfere, all right. The Byrds need to know that their decisions affect more than just the few of them."

He left Hugh sitting on the bench while he scraped off his plate into a receptacle and then headed for the main house, where the dim lights buttered the back windows in the falling dusk.

And where Donna Byrd was about to get an earful.

Needing privacy, Donna had come outside to the wraparound porch, where she sat on the new cottage-style swing she and the girls had chosen for the renovation.

*Just do this,* she thought, looking at the cell phone in her hand. *Go. Now. Dial!*

But she couldn't, even if Dad and Uncle William had finally checked in this morning with their own votes after one heck of a long night of waiting.

They both wanted to find James. And they were both evidently done with their Hill Country trip, on their way back to their respective homes in Houston and Uncle William's ranch. Even the most clueless person in the world could infer that there'd been a setback with the brothers because of last night's news, but Donna and the rest of her relatives had promised each other that they would do everything within their power to make things right between them again.

Yet there was *this* to deal with, as well. And, since Donna had been riding their P.I.'s tail this whole time about Savannah and a possible child, she was the one who'd volunteered to give him the go ahead on tracking down James.

Still, the phone was incredibly heavy in her hand, almost as if it was something that could drag her down until she wouldn't ever be able to get back up.

Was she going to let one phone call beat her, though?

She dialed without another thought, listening to one ring. Two.

Then, an answer.

"Walker Investigations," said the P.I.'s rusty-nail voice.

"Hi, Roland, it's Donna Byrd."

"Miss Byrd—I haven't heard from you for a whole day. I thought you might've dropped off the face of the planet."

Hilarious. "We were only waiting for our dads to weigh in on Savannah and James."

"And?"

She closed her eyes, opened them. "We'd like you to go forward on finding out more about James and setting up a possible meeting."

"Consider it done." She could hear Roland tapping on a keyboard. "What about Savannah?"

"Right…Savannah."

Donna bit her lip before giving a real answer. Last night, the Byrd children had discussed James's mom, too, after they had called their dads and then met in the living room again. That's when Donna had told them

what she'd left out during their first gathering—news
about Savannah Jeffries that just hadn't seemed as important as the more urgent revelation of James; facts
such as how Savannah was a very successful interior
designer with her own business and how she was going
by her late husband's last name and how it seemed that
she had gotten married long after James Bowie Jeffries
had come of legal age, hence the reason he used his
mom's maiden name.

So *much* information. And so much conflict, because
after Donna had filled in the family, they'd been just as
divided as ever—this time about including Savannah
in a reunion.

Donna sighed. No turning back now. "If you could
go ahead and contact Savannah, we want to invite her
to meet us, as well."

It would be a smash-up family reunion, emphasis on
the *smash-up*.

After she took care of particulars with Roland, then
hung up, she stayed on the swing.

Dammit, she only wished she had zero interest in Savannah. But she had voted yes both times last night, and
part of the reason was because the idea of the woman
just wouldn't leave Donna alone. She was everything
Donna had ever looked for in her role models—obviously ambitious, based on her business skills. Donna also
liked that she knew how to decorate a room—a hobby
that she, herself, had recently turned into somewhat of
a vocation with the B and B.

Most of all, though, Donna respected that, from what
she knew, Savannah had raised James by herself.

*An independent woman in every way,* she thought.

And even though she hadn't planned on ever having a family herself…

Well, there was an empty place in Donna that actually perked up at the thought, now that she finally *did* have a family she was starting to feel closer and closer to.

But really? Her? The überprofessional Donna Byrd?

A mom?

It would've been laughable if there wasn't a string of yearning tying her up because of the lingering notion.

The wind stirred and, from the side of the porch, she could hear some chimes tinkling. The sound reminded her of a soothing song that a baby mobile might make above a crib. Someday.

Maybe.

The porch swing was creaking back and forth in a lazy rhythm when Donna saw someone coming around the side of the house.

And guess who?

But instead of groaning with exasperation, her heart gave a jaunty flip.

Oddly, though, Caleb Granger's grin wasn't as dimply as usual. And she could've used one of his sexy grins right about now.

She spoke first, just as he began to mount the porch steps, coming into the light from the caged lantern near the door.

"Are you here to say a good evening to me?"

He stopped near the top, his hands planted on his hips. "I heard some talk, so I thought I'd come over to let you confirm or deny the rumors."

Whatever kind of peaceful bubble she'd just created for herself busted like a balloon.

"Rumors?" she asked tightly.

"About the new Byrd. About all the arguing you and your family were doing about him."

"Maybe the next time we Byrds have a conversation," she said, "we can broadcast it to the entire ranch. Do you know anything about installing closed-circuit television?"

He ignored her sarcasm. "Just listen to me on this. For years, this ranch has been what you might call 'harmonious.' Tex made sure everyone was happy, inside and outside the main house. He even went the extra mile at the end of his life to guarantee that his family made amends with each other, and it's a damned shame that all his hard work seems to be for naught."

Donna couldn't say a word. Not *one*. Anger was roiling in her…and maybe even something else. She'd never had a man presume to talk to her like this. She'd never stood for someone to so boldly nose into her business.

But…*damn* whatever it was weaving around all that anger in her. It was something that had her utterly confused, and she struck out in an effort to erase it.

"Is your lecture over now?" she asked. "Because I'm already bored."

*"Bored?"*

He narrowed his gaze, and she did the same right back at him.

"Yes," she said. "Bored. You know why? Because I have a hundred other issues all poking at me from every side, and yours don't even begin to compete with them."

He took a moment, looking down at the porch, as if to compose himself. Then he let out a curt laugh.

She didn't know what to make of that.

"Believe it or not," he said, "I'm only looking out for

Tex's interests. Do you know what it would've done to him if he'd heard y'all arguing?"

"There's more going on than even Tex knew."

Caleb locked gazes with her, reading her, and she stiffened. But she also melted ever so slightly, deep in her core, where she never melted.

He cared. She could see that. But she didn't want his care, didn't want anyone to meddle because she and Jenna and their cousins would have this under control soon.

She rested her hands flat on the swing, leaning forward. "I told you before—I know how close you were to Tex, but that doesn't mean—"

"Sometimes I wonder if you Byrds have any idea what Tex gave to you, what he did for you."

Donna felt her face go pale, and she knew that *he* knew he was wrong.

He gentled his tone. "What I'm trying to ask you to do is to stop battling with each other and appreciate what you have. That's all he would've wanted."

He said it with such longing that her heart bumped against her ribs.

But her anger had been fully roused, and her voice was torn when she answered.

"I know what I have now, believe me, because I didn't have much of it before."

Before now, her life had been defined by a father who was all business, plus a mom who hadn't been alive for years and whom Donna had missed so much that she had told herself to never put her heart out there again, where it could be stomped all over.

When Caleb took a step onto the porch, one booted foot still on the stair behind him, Donna didn't move.

Was he coming up here to get his point across even more emphatically?

But he didn't advance. Instead, he slipped his thumbs into his belt loops, a sheepish look on his face.

"Sorry for laying into you like that," he said. "I didn't realize how seriously you were taking this."

"As seriously as you do, evidently." *Breathe, just breathe.*

But when he came all the way up onto the porch, breathing wasn't easy. Plus, he was making her skin do funny things, raising goose bumps and causing her fine hairs to stand on end.

If he noticed the evidence on her bare arms, he didn't say anything.

"Promise me you'll let me know if you need help with any of this mess," he said.

"I've got it covered."

Brother, did *he* have a lot to learn about her.

His voice lowered. "I'm being serious. Just give a yell if you need me for anything."

She wasn't sure they were talking about family business anymore.

"Thanks, but no thanks." She rose from the swing, and it creaked, as if in protest.

As she passed him on her way to the door, she smelled that saddle soap on his skin, and it filled her head, making her dizzy.

A chuckle stopped her in her tracks, and she glanced over her shoulder to find him shaking his head.

"What?" she asked.

"You're what we call a 'firebrand' out here."

"I guess that just means if you insist on getting in my business anymore, you're going to get burned."

He laughed, and the dimples made a grand appearance, tweaking her heart with sparks that showered down until they settled in her belly.

But just as quickly, she shoved the ridiculous feelings aside.

Not her type. Never would be. And just as soon as she got back to the city, it'd be much easier to remember that fact.

As if he had sensed the direction of her thoughts, he gave her another one of those sultry up-and-down looks, sweeping her skin with flame.

When he got to her eyes, his gaze snagged hers with an electric jolt.

"Thought about that wine yet, Donna Byrd?"

She rolled her eyes, opening the front door and going through it, hearing his laughter while she leaned back against the wood.

And, damn it all if she couldn't help the smile that wouldn't leave her alone afterward.

The weekend was ushered in with a blast of July heat, and even after the sun started to dive down to the horizon, it was sweaty business.

But the misters and fans that had been planted around the yard near the side of the barn helped, as Caleb spread a blanket over the grass and put down an ice-filled bucket that held a bottle of rosé.

The other night, when he had confronted Donna about the Byrd-fight rumors, he'd left on a better note than the one he'd come to her on. And tonight, Donna Byrd was going to have that wine with him so they could completely make up...whether she knew it or not.

Manny and Maria were just coming from the buffet line, where the cook was dishing out the food to the staff and their children.

"Lookee here," Manny said, one hand holding a plate loaded with barbecue and all the trimmings, the other hand holding Maria's. "Someone's getting romantic with themselves."

Caleb reached into the bucket for a piece of ice and flicked it at his coworker. Maria laughed until Manny offered Caleb a rascally smile and pulled her away to their lawn chairs, which were closer to the makeshift screen that Donna had hung from the side of the barn.

Even though other female staff members cruised by Caleb, grinning at him, maybe even expecting him to revert to form and do some flirting, he wasn't swayed. He patiently went back to waiting for Donna to appear and, when she finally did, his hormones went into overdrive, growling like a roadster before a race.

White summery sundress, strappy sandals, blond hair twisted and pinned so that her neck was bare…Donna Byrd slayed him and, as usual, he couldn't take his eyes off her.

Except when he saw the man she was with.

It was as if Caleb's engine sputtered. Her "friend from college" who was supposed to be here to write an article did indeed carry an expensive camera with him, aiming it around the area. And if this pricey accessory wasn't enough, he had an East Coast crustiness about him, dressed in brand-spanking-new jeans and a short-sleeved plaid shirt that marked him as a dude. He even had yacht-boy hair, light blond and flipped up in front, as if it was gelled to within an inch of its life.

When Caleb saw him and Donna across the lawn, laughing together at some private joke, he wondered if he should've read more into the moment when she'd told him about this "friend."

Of course a knockout like her would have "friends."

But a niggle of doubt still hounded Caleb, although he did have the feeling that tonight really might not be the time for getting Donna to leave her buddy and sit down to drink some wine with him.

He glanced at the bottle and at the glasses. Hell, why let a good vintage go to waste?

He reached into the bucket to pull out the wine just as Tina Crandall, the elderly housekeeper who stood out in a crowd with her silver-streaked black hair, strolled by.

Everyone knew Tina enjoyed a splash of spirits every now and then, so he whistled, and when she turned around, he lifted up a glass to her.

Her gaze sparkled. "You devil. What do you have here?"

"A Domaine Tempier rosé." He'd driven to the suburbs during the week after a full day of work to visit his aunt and his father. It'd gone as it usually did, with Dad loudly complaining about dinner, and the highlight of Caleb's night had been dropping by a store farther over in Houston to buy this bottle.

Tina gingerly sat on the blanket, spreading her flowered skirt around her ample hips. "That sounds like a fancy label, Caleb. I think Tex would've loved it."

"Then let's drink to him."

He poured a glass for her, then himself. They toasted and drank to Tex.

After they took that first sip, he kept his eye on Donna as she and the yacht boy passed close to the barn. When she seemed to hold back a sneeze, he recalled hearing that she occasionally took allergy medicine whenever she absolutely had to spend time near any hay.

Hell, she was taking one for the team tonight.

Tina drank some more, being ladylike and discreet about it, but Caleb didn't have much taste for the wine tonight. All he could do was percolate as Donna and her friend walked around the area, still laughing and touching each other's arms.

Full darkness—and movie time—arrived, and Donna Byrd and Gilligan went to some reserved lawn chairs. But, first, the guy took flash pictures of people enjoying their food while waiting for the film.

When Donna strolled by Caleb's blanket by herself, her gaze met his. He toasted her with his nearly full glass, then reached over to refill Tina's.

"Looks like you brought the wine, after all," Donna Byrd said casually. A nearby mister blew a strand of hair out of her upswept 'do, and the tendril caressed her neck.

Caleb's fingers itched to do the same. "If I had an extra glass, I'd pour some for you, but I gather you're busy."

Tina obviously had a buzz on, and she grabbed the neck of the bottle, pouring even more into her glass. "You're missing some good stuff, Donna."

She smiled at the housekeeper, but just as she was about to turn her attention to Caleb, her friend meandered over with his camera, snapping a picture of Caleb and Tina on the blanket.

Caleb pulled down the brim of his hat, discouraging any more of that nonsense.

Donna linked arms with Jimmy Olsen. "Theo, this is Tina, who runs the household. And this is Caleb, one of the hands here."

Theo bent down to shake Tina's hand, then Caleb's. "You both run a good operation. Donna and the girls have got a real gem on their hands with this B and B idea."

When he straightened back up and wrapped an arm around Donna's shoulder, Caleb just about rocketed off the blanket.

But he kept his hat on. Literally. And he offered a vague smile to the dude.

Donna linked arms with her boy pal, and for a bright second, Caleb wondered if she was being deft, avoiding what had obviously been an attempt to cuddle.

"Have fun," she said to Caleb and Tina, then strolled away with her guest.

Caleb kept watching them from under his hat, especially when Donna sneaked a glance back at him.

But what did that mean? And what was with the arm linking?

He was still wondering that when the movie flashed onto the screen, much to the delight of the crowd, who applauded and hooted as the title of *The Man from Snowy River* appeared.

And when Caleb saw Donna seating Theo in a chair of honor right in the center of things, then excuse herself, he couldn't hold his questions any longer.

He leaned over to Tina, who'd turned the empty wine bottle upside down in the bucket. "I'll be back."

"Take your time," she said with a happy lilt as she watched the screen.

He followed Donna to the back of the house, where the new bucking bronco fountain splashed playfully.

And where she sprawled in a cushioned chair, her white skirt hanging down like angel's wings.

His heart caught in his chest as he stood there, taking her in, his body going warm.

Tired Donna. Beautiful Donna.

Maybe this was just lust, but Caleb wasn't so sure about that. There was something chemical between them he couldn't explain and, more than anything, he wanted to see why he always found himself coming to her when most women came to him.

He sat on a wood bench nearby, taking care to make enough noise so that he didn't scare her, and when she glanced over, she put her palm to her chest, as if to keep her heart from leaping out of it.

It was like the moment he'd initially laid eyes on her all over again—attraction at first sight.

And maybe something more?

## Chapter Four

Why wouldn't Donna's heart calm down around Caleb Granger?

She'd never been this flustered by any man before—not when one sent her a drink during happy hour in a dimly lit bar, not when one locked gazes with her in Central Park on the weekends, when she would lounge on a blanket and bask in the summer sun with a good book.

Was it dark enough to hide the blush that she suspected had consumed her?

Right. *A blush*. That had to be another first for her. But, then again, why not? She'd been sitting here by the fountain, thinking about Caleb, and he'd suddenly appeared like a tempting devil that never gave her a moment of peace.

It would help if he didn't look so mouthwatering as he sat on that bench, an angle of light from the nearby patio revealing the sparkle in his pale blue eyes and the dimpled barely there grin. Not even that ever-present cowboy hat could hide his charms.

"What are you doing here?" she asked.

"I live on this ranch, remember?"

"You know that's not what I mean." It seemed she was always getting her wires crossed with him. This time, all he'd done was show up where she was, and it was enough to… Well, *fluster* her. "I meant to ask why you're not watching the movie with everyone else."

"I'm not so much the movie sort." He shrugged, sitting back on the bench, propping his booted ankle on his knee and nudging back the brim of his hat with his knuckles. "I don't see the use in watching someone else's fictional life go by when I've got a perfectly good and real one myself."

A curious little bug inside of her wanted to ask what he did do for entertainment. Read books? Go on a computer? But that would mean she was interested.

And she wasn't.

"I'm afraid a movie is all the amusement that's being offered tonight," she said. "Unless you came here to stare at this fountain, too."

"That's as perfect an excuse as any." He looked at the bronze bronco sculpture covered by running water. "It's peaceful. But I'm sure that's why you came over here. To get some peace."

"It has been a long day."

She leaned her head back on the wicker chair's cushion, and a breath escaped her. She didn't intend to give so much away with that sigh, though.

"More family stuff?" he asked, his tone a surprisingly serene distraction for her. It didn't hold the judgmental edge she'd detected in him the other night, when he'd confronted her on the main house's porch about how the Byrds were handling ranch business.

She found herself talking. "The family's just on pins and needles waiting for a call from our P.I."

"Did he approach Savannah or James about meeting with you?"

"Yes, but he hasn't gotten word from either of them so far." She paused. "It certainly wasn't an easy decision to ask him to go forward with this."

"Meeting either one of them will change everyone's lives. I can imagine it wasn't easy."

He lapsed into silence, and it gave way to the trickle of water from the fountain and the sounds of the summer Texas night—crickets and a hundred other things a city girl like her couldn't identify yet.

It was nice that he seemed to sympathize with her family's problems, but now would be a good time to stop revealing her emotions to him. Truthfully, there was a lot more bothering Donna than Savannah and James. She'd also gotten an email from her financial advisor this morning, letting her know that her portfolio was in sadder shape than the last time she'd checked in with him.

But wasn't that news just the sprinkles on top of the crumbling cupcake of her life?

Caleb shifted in his seat, and that strange tingly sensation Donna felt whenever she was around him traced the lining of her stomach again.

"You left your 'friend' all alone to watch the movie," he said.

She sneaked a sideways glance at him. He was trying to look casual after asking the question. That almost made her smile.

"Is that why you plopped down on that bench?" she

asked, amusement coloring her tone. "So you could quiz me about Theo?"

He shrugged again, oh so carelessly.

Was the cowboy jealous?

She recalled how he had watched her walk away with Theo as she led her guest to his movie seat. Caleb had been wearing a burning look that had flipped her tummy inside out, making her all too aware that she shouldn't have been glancing back at him in the first place.

Had she *wanted* to see if he was curious about Theo?

Caleb tipped back his hat even more, and she caught the side-slant grin on his face now. "This Theo fellow is sure your type."

"What do you mean, my type?"

"It looks like he walked straight off of the Queen of England's polo field with those perfect pants and that hair of his."

Now Donna did laugh. "His hair does have a glamorous life of its own."

"That's not what I'm trying to get at, Donna."

She could tell he'd become serious because he hadn't added the playful "Byrd" to her name. Also, he had leaned forward, planting both boots on the ground and his forearms on his thighs.

She wasn't going to ask what he was getting at. No, she would end this civil conversation and then go back to check on Theo and the movie. That way, she wouldn't encourage Caleb any more than he'd obviously been encouraged by that glance she'd given him while walking away with Theo.

Dammit, why hadn't she been able to keep herself from checking out his reaction to her leaving?

"I told you," she said. "Theo's a friend. We met at

NYU. He even married one of my sorority sisters and they've been going on eight years together."

At the word *married,* Caleb's grin had reappeared.

It goaded Donna. "He isn't the only man I know from New York. And the others are of the single variety."

"How many of those *do* you know?"

*Now* was the time to make sure he realized that he had no chance with her. "Enough to keep me occupied."

He chuckled, and she crossed one leg over the other, leaning away from him.

"Well, Donna Byrd," he said, "you seem to have a real good life to get back to after you take care of this B and B here in Texas. I hear you'll be able to market the place from a distance."

See—he was getting her drift. "It's an ideal situation."

"So you're looking forward to getting back to all the traffic and crowds."

"Believe it or not, all of that is just as natural to me as everything on this ranch is to you."

"From what I hear, your sister's not the same as you are. She's taken to the Flying B like a swan to water."

"It sounds like you're asking in a roundabout way why she turned out one way and I turned out another."

He cocked an eyebrow, keeping his gaze on her, causing another stunningly pleasant shiver to travel her skin.

Donna didn't see the harm in briefly talking about Jenna. "She grew up with a fascination about country life because of a deep curiosity she had about Grandpa and his side of the family, since Dad never talked about either of them."

"He didn't?"

"No." Donna smoothed her skirt over a leg. "You know the story, though—how Savannah came between my dad and my uncle William and how the situation estranged them from Grandpa. As I said, Jenna wondered about Grandpa, but so did I, even though I never said much about it or acted on it. Dad discouraged any interest, and I worshipped the ground he walked on, so I listened to him when he said that there was a big world out there to explore and I shouldn't bother myself about his side of the family."

Once again, he'd gotten her to talk more than she'd meant to. How did Caleb Granger manage to do that?

And why did it feel okay to finally be releasing some of the weight that had been perching on her for months now?

He sat still, and she could tell that he wasn't happy about how Sam had turned his back on Tex. She didn't reveal that, in the end, she wasn't so happy about it, either.

So much time wasted. So much opportunity squandered.

She decided to go on…just a little bit more. Then she would leave.

"Jenna was different from me in a lot of ways," she said, "and she decided to embrace the Byrds' roots, with or without knowing Grandpa. It was almost as if she was born to be here."

Donna stopped herself before adding, *And I wasn't.*

As the fountain splashed, she wondered if it was so easy to go on about this because Caleb had been close to Tex. Was she looking for someone who knew Grandpa well to forgive her for not seeking out this ranch and her family?

Guilt found its way to her again as she thought of how Grandpa's gaze had lit up the first time they'd met, and how she wished, too late, that she'd gotten a lifetime full of those looks over the years, even though she would rather hide that wish than tell anyone about it.

"So that's why you forged a path to the city," Caleb finally said. "Because of your dad's influence."

"I would say he was instrumental in that."

She glanced back toward where the movie was playing. In the near distance, she could hear the sound track's music.

But Caleb wasn't done with her. "I also heard that you got some kind of internship, then a job at a magazine after college. One of those sophisticated ladies' publications."

He'd said it almost in a kidding way, as if emphasizing that she was one of those ladies.

"You've done some homework on us new Byrds," she said.

"Word gets around." He paused, then said, "A few years ago, you had an idea for a start-up publication, and you had your own magazine for a while."

Donna pressed her lips together, her chin tilting up a little.

"That takes some guts, Donna Byrd," Caleb said softly. "Bringing something big into the world like that."

The genuine admiration in his voice made her hesitate. When she saw how he was looking at her—straightforward, direct—it stirred her up, heated her to the very core.

He slowly got to his feet and, once again, something in Donna's chest was sparked to electric life, leaving a heated friction to trail down her body.

"I know," he said in that same low tone, "that you have new opportunities nowadays. You're going to turn this B and B into a rousing success, and you think you'll run back to the city after that. You think you're going to get your old life going again."

"I *think* I will?" she asked, and her voice didn't come out as strongly as she would've liked.

He took a couple of steps toward her, his boots thudding on the cement.

Every sound was like a contradiction to all her plans. What he wasn't saying outright was that she had a career here, if she wanted it. She had the family she'd never had before, right in front of her for the taking.

And she had other opportunities, as well....

Caleb took another few steps, until he was standing in front of her chair. She still couldn't move.

"If I were a betting man," he said, "I'd put money on the notion that you won't be going anywhere after this, Donna Byrd."

"After...what?"

"After you give everything on the Flying B a chance," he said, his voice so sensual that it glided over her skin like water sluicing down the smooth contours of the fountain.

He took his damned time bending down, bracing his hands on either arm of her chair and, oh, God, he smelled so good—saddle soap and only enough hint of hay to make her think she might not be allergic to this ranch after all.

Her head swam, making her thoughts race by in a whir of sensation. Adrenaline zipped through her, a shot to the heart.

Was he going to kiss her? This cowboy who had no place in her life?

As he bent lower, she closed her eyes, her lips buzzing with anticipation.

But, beneath her eyelids, everything she'd ever wanted rushed by: bright neon lights zigging and zagging, laughter and the sound of clinking glasses from crowded rooms, her favorite fountain in Central Park, splashing....

The sound of her memories melded with the present, and she heard another fountain instead—this one, here in Texas.

She opened her eyes, holding her breath while she slipped under one of his arms and came to a stand by the side of her chair. Her heartbeat was throttling her now.

He glanced over his shoulder at her, his eyebrow raised. But it seemed like he was more amused than surprised.

"You move fast," he said.

"I think the same could be said for you."

Another chuckle from him.

Even if her body was responding with a runaway pulse that kept her breathless, this wasn't what she needed. Him. Just another piece of trouble to add to all the crazy emotions that were attacking her day by day with Savannah and James and the insanity of her entire life. There were men back in New York who would be far more suited for her—men who fit into the existence she was made for.

She flailed for something to say. "I like movies."

Articulate? Hardly. But it made Caleb straighten up ever so slowly from her former seat, anyway.

"So you do," he said.

"What I mean is that you don't like them. I do. And that's just one glaring difference between us."

"Ah." He adjusted his hat, then negligently rested his hands on his jeaned hips. "You're talking me out of wanting to kiss you."

Good—once again he'd caught on. "I'm also used to men who are a little more subtle, by the way."

"Fellows in fancy suits and ties and slicked-back hair? I wouldn't call them subtle, just well-disguised."

"What do you mean by that?"

"A man's a man. But some of us don't hide behind fancy words or twenty-dollar cocktails that we buy in the hopes of winning a woman over."

She crossed her arms over her chest, yet it was only because of the goose bumps that had risen over her arms, prickling her skin. Good goose bumps that seeped through her, arousing her when that should've been the last thing happening.

"I think there's another way to describe the kind of men I usually associate with," Donna said. "It's called *couth.* Instead of stealing kisses, those men ask a woman out on a date, get to know her over a nice dinner."

"I'll bet I already know more about you than any of your couth men ever did."

"Doubtful."

Yet, even as she said it, she realized that he might be right. She'd never gotten serious with any of those dates in the city—not emotionally, anyway. There'd just never been time.

Or, if she was honest with herself, she'd never been as interested in a man as she had been in seeing to the success of her magazine.

But here, on the Flying B, she was another Donna, wasn't she? And Caleb had gotten a glimpse of her.

And he *still* wanted to kiss her....

When he finally spoke, he had become serious again. "I don't know if *couth* describes me, but it seems you're working under some wrong impressions, at any rate."

"Like what?"

"Like mistaking why I might want to be around you. Did it ever occur to you that I'm trying to figure out just what it is about you that impressed me in the first place?"

She waited for it—the inevitable glance at her chest, her curves. And, somehow, she was already disappointed that Caleb wouldn't be much different from the rest of the men she'd gone out with.

But his gaze was still on her face. "I've seen a lot of pretty girls, but there's something about you that sets you apart."

"You could tell that just by looking at me one time?"

"Could be." He smiled. "Could be that I could tell right off that you didn't take guff from anyone, and that appealed to me. I've never met a woman who keeps me on my toes like you do. And there's a lot more to you, too, Donna. A lot that you don't seem to want anyone to see."

She tried not to show how much he'd just stunned her with his all-too-keen observation.

But he'd obviously said what he'd come here to say, even if he hadn't gotten a kiss out of it. He tipped his hat to her, then walked away without any more explanation.

She watched him go, unable to tear her gaze away.

Unable to figure out just why *he* got to *her* more than any man ever had before.

Caleb had spent the night staring at the ceiling of his cabin, trying to puzzle out the enigma that was Donna Byrd.

And trying to answer that ever-elusive question of just *why* he couldn't get her off his mind.

He'd never believed in fairy dust and magic of the heart, but he did believe in the chemistry one person had with another—and he knew he had something like that with Donna. He really hadn't been stringing her along when he'd said that she kept him on his toes. No woman had ever challenged him like that before—and it pleased him that Donna, who came from a world with art museums and theater to keep her stimulated, seemed to be on her toes with him, too.

During the past year, Caleb had gotten an earful, listening to his dad telling him how useless he was, thanks to the dementia as well as the knowledge that his dad had probably felt like that for years but kept it to himself when Mom was alive. So half of Caleb had started to believe he was simple and would never amount to much. Of course, Tex's belief in him had changed some of that, but there'd still been a lingering suspicion that his dad was right.

Yet how could he keep up with a bright, sophisticated woman like Donna if any of that were true? He might not like movies and he might not wear ironed yuppie shirts and trust-fund hair like Theo, but Caleb instinctively knew that he affected her in a way that she wasn't used to when it came to men.

When he'd nearly kissed her, he'd seen her get all hot and bothered. He'd also seen some kind of vulnerability in her that he'd noticed before, as if, below her surface, she was far more than the superficial cosmopolitan woman who'd found herself stuck in the country.

*Chemistry,* he'd thought, before finally getting to

sleep. It was only part of what he suspected there could be with Donna....

By morning, he knew what his next step should be with her.

After a day mainly spent bathing and grooming horses, he headed straight for his cabin to clean himself up, then went to the main house's kitchen and sweet-talked Barbara out of a few ingredients from the pantry, as well as some of the fresh-baked bread and apple pie she'd made for dinner. Then he went to the place everyone called "the dream cabin," since it would suit his purposes just fine for the night.

Back in the day, Tex had used all the cabins around the property to entertain guests at the big parties he'd thrown—but that had been before Savannah had come around. After she'd broken up the family, the cabins had been abandoned until the Byrd women had revived them for their B and B. They'd decorated this particular building with a sheepskin throw over the brown quilted bed—the so-called magic mattress that had given the cabin its "dream" nickname. The room also had birchwood accents, lending the feel of a cozy retreat.

In the small kitchen, he prepared a salad, seasoned mushrooms and two rib-eye steaks, and as they sizzled in a skillet, he grabbed the clothing bag he'd draped over a chair and pulled out the nicest suit he had. After turning off the stove, tossing his cowboy hat on the bed and then getting dressed, he knotted a tie at his throat, picked up his phone and texted Donna's cell number, which he'd finagled from Barbara, too.

Something's cooking in the dream cabin. You might want to check it out.

He could've predicted Donna's response.

Who is this?

He answered with a lone question mark, then put his phone away.

If there was one more thing he would've guessed about Donna, it was that she wouldn't ignore such a message, especially about the dream cabin, which had been so integral to the story of Savannah and the Byrds.

During the time he estimated it might take Donna to get down here, he was able to spread a cloth over the small table in the tiny kitchen, light a candle, scoop the food onto plates, plus pour two glasses of Cabernet Sauvignon that he'd already decanted. Tex had once given him a dozen bottles of red from his cellar, and Caleb had been keeping them for a night like this.

When Donna arrived, she opened the door, then stood stock-still while Caleb tried not to let his heart get the better of him. She was wearing a filmy, flowery sundress with elegant, flat, strappy sandals, and her light hair was up, revealing the neck that he'd fantasized about kissing time and again.

"What's going on with you now?" she asked while eyeing the candle on the table, the wine, the food.

His suit.

"I'm taking you out to dinner tonight. Or maybe I should say that I'm bringing dinner to you, since I highly doubt you would've gone to any restaurants with me."

Her mouth shaped into yet another question— *"What?"*—but it never quite came out, because he interrupted her by holding up a hand.

"Don't tell me you don't like wine. I made some steaks, too."

"It's just that I don't remember making a date with you, Caleb."

"You didn't."

"Especially not in the dream cabin."

"I knew that if you got a text inviting you to my own place, you wouldn't go near it. This cabin is neutral ground."

"Then—"

He didn't allow her the chance to squirm out of this. "Last night, you said I was different from the men you usually meet. I don't think that's the case. You need subtle? Well, I can provide the suit, some cocktails and then dinner, just like anyone else."

She was shaking her head, but she didn't look as pissed at him as he expected she might be.

"I don't know what to say."

"A 'yes' would suffice. You don't even have to change clothes. You're already dressed for an evening out."

Okay, she didn't look pissed at all, just confused now. Once again, he thought she might be wondering if he was an alien from planet Loco.

Then she broke into a clearly reluctant smile. "You did go through some trouble."

"I wanted to show you that—"

"I was wrong about you. That's abundantly clear by now." She sighed. "And you're going to keep on trying to prove your point until I give in, aren't you?"

She was wrong about *that*. "No, I won't. If you want to go, then you should. But I would like you to sit down here to see that there's more to us in Buckshot Hills than meets the eye."

He could detect the battle in her gaze—should she sit down or shouldn't she?—and it heartened him a little.

Then she put the kibosh on that. "I don't know. I was planning on having Barbara fix me a plate for my room because I've got a lot of work to do."

"Is your magazine friend Theo still here?"

"No. He spent the day with Tammy and Jenna showing him the outdoor activities we'll have on the ranch, but he left this afternoon."

"Then there's always work that'll be waiting, Donna."

This seemed to make her think twice, and he saw that vulnerability—or was it loneliness?—in her gaze that he'd seen before.

"I'm tempted to say yes," she said softly, "just so you can see that a night out with me wouldn't be what you expected."

"Then prove *your* point to *me*."

She met his gaze square-on, obviously making a decision.

Lifting a finger, she said, "This is the only time this is going to happen."

"Good enough."

While she slowly made her way toward the table, as if he was going to pounce on her and she needed to be on her guard, she surveyed him in his suit. His body rushed with a flood of heat, because it was an appreciative look, whether she'd meant it to be or not.

He went to pull her chair out for her, and she sat. Then he set a filled wineglass in front of her.

"I didn't realize that you can cook," she said.

"There're times when the skill comes in handy." He'd done a lot of cooking during his leave of absence from the ranch, when he'd gotten Aunt Rosemary and Dad settled into their new home. Rosemary had needed the break.

He didn't want to think about that, though—not with Donna so near, her lemon-drop perfume tickling his senses.

"Is it too old-fashioned for a man to cook?" he asked, taking his own seat. "Or is it a sign of the kind of modern man you think I'm not?"

She ignored his question as she sipped her wine. "Mmm. This is good."

He toasted her with his glass and, as if she were giving him a well-earned point, she did the same, then drank more.

After she put her glass down, she took up her fork. "I think it's only fair that I be clear about things, Caleb. Very clear."

He waited her out.

"You seem to believe that I'm looking for something that I'm not looking for."

"Like a constant man in your life?"

"Yes, something like that."

Well, maybe he was hoping for that.

And, by the end of the night, he was going to do everything within his power to change her mind about being a single city girl.

## Chapter Five

So far, this "date" or whatever it was with Caleb Granger wasn't quite the disaster Donna had thought it would be.

Then again, what had she been expecting? For them to be at a loss for something to talk about? For the date to be so awkward that the sky would fall down on them?

Neither seemed to be happening...

So far.

He was breaking off a piece of sourdough bread from a loaf in a basket. "Since we're in the process of being clear with each other, I'd like to add something to the conversation we were having last night. You asked me why I was drawn to you and you didn't seem satisfied with the answer I gave you."

Straightforward as always.

He buttered the bread. "It's no secret that, when you Byrds first came to the ranch, stories circulated about your family. And those stories piqued my interest. Especially about you."

"What did they all say? That I was stuck-up? That I could destroy anyone with a withering glance?" She laughed. "*I* heard you're a ladies' man who likes a good chase, but I'm surprised that even the most experienced Casanova would want to go through the trouble of dealing with an ice queen."

He gave her a slanted grin, and for a moment, with him dressed up in his suit and with his dark blond hair tamed, her heart fluttered.

Then he said, "They did say you were a blonde bombshell, but that's not what interested me the most."

"Really."

"All right," he said. "I was curious about whether you lived up to the descriptions. And you do."

*Blush.*

She had to learn how not to do that around him.

"But," he said, "as I mentioned before, I liked the idea of how damned independent you were. Some men admire a woman who knows herself and doesn't necessarily need anyone else."

*Did* she know what she was about?

She brushed the question aside and played with a mushroom on her plate with her fork. "Just as I thought— you like the idea of a chase. It sounds like you created a bit of a fantasy about me."

"Maybe I did. And maybe part of your appeal was in the idea of what it might be like for me to eventually be a part of the Byrd family, too…."

She sat there, stunned, as he stopped abruptly.

Had he just admitted that he wasn't merely trying to

date her—he'd had much bigger fantasies in mind that had to do with marrying into her family?

As the shock wore off, she realized that he looked unsettled, as if he regretted what he'd said. But more to the point, she wondered if his tone had been a bit wistful, too.

*Had* his fantasy involved officially being like a son to Tex, if her grandfather had lived longer?

"Well," she said, easing the tension. "So much for fantasies. You've probably intuited that I'm not the marrying type."

His gaze was stalwart, solid, as it met hers again, whipping her into a silent frenzy before she got hold of herself.

"As usual," he said, "that came out the wrong way. I didn't mean for you to think that I was attracted to you because of your family ties. It was just something that'd crossed my mind long after I saw you."

She wasn't going to give him hell for this. She actually believed him. "I understand how you might still want to feel close to Tex through the Byrds, and why dating one of his granddaughters seems like a good idea."

He laid down his fork, and the candlelight flitted over his tanned skin, reflecting a lone flame in his pale blue eyes. "I can't say enough how much Tex and the rest of the people on this ranch meant to me."

What was Caleb's family like that he felt as if he had more of one here?

Donna didn't want to ask questions. She didn't want to get that deep.

"You don't have to explain this to me," she said.

"I should, after putting my foot in my mouth like

that." He shrugged. "See, I don't have what you'd call a perfect relationship with my own dad."

"You took a leave of absence to be with him, right? At least, that's what I heard."

He nodded. "My parents never had any other children, so I'm really the only one besides my aunt Rosemary who can take care of Dad. He's got dementia, and Rosemary tries her best, but it's a lot to ask of her. Even before he needed care, though, we weren't the closest."

Maybe it was the dormant journalist in her, but she ended up asking, "What about your mom?"

"She had an accident in the house one day, using a ladder to clean a high bookshelf, falling. It was just after I graduated high school and left home."

Maybe Donna did have a few things in common with Caleb, after all. "I'm sorry to hear that. My mom died when I was nine. I know what it's like to grow up without her around."

"It's like half of you disappears, and there's no way to replace that part of you, isn't it?"

Donna nodded, not wanting to say anything else, because Mom's cancer had meant that she and Jenna had needed to go live with Dad. Their parents had been divorced by that time, and she and Jenna normally saw him only on the weekends. He'd had a very different philosophy of child-rearing than their mother, raising Donna and Jenna to organize their lives as they would a business. And why not, when the most successful thing Dad had ever been was a businessman?

Even though Donna hadn't been as close to her mom as she should've been—another regret—she'd never felt so numb as she had after her death. That's when she'd realized that emotional distance—her dad's practice—was the easiest way to go about living.

"How's your dad doing?" Donna asked.

"These days, he barely even recognizes me. And when he does, he lets me know how happy he is to have Aunt Rosemary taking care of him instead of his 'irresponsible kid.'" He laughed a little. "At least, back when I was younger, he didn't outright tell me how much he disliked me."

Donna frowned. "It stinks that you have to go through that."

"It is what it is."

"Besides, you don't sound all that irresponsible to me. Maybe a little…impulsive…but—"

"I had my days of hell-raising, believe me. I wrecked two trucks because I had a foot of lead, and I can't even count how many times I ended up in the principal's office. Dad was never amused, and that's the kid he remembers most times."

Something was chipping away at Donna's chest, as if trying to get inside, but she picked up her glass and drank. The wine slid down her throat, warm and soothing, chasing away everything that was trying to get to her.

Caleb had moved on, though. He grinned as he said, "You know—if my dad could see me setting my sights on one woman like I've done with you, he might look at me a different way on his lucid days."

He was back to teasing her, maybe because the conversation had gotten a bit heavy.

She said, "How many ways can I tell you that I'm the last person you should even think of settling down with?"

"You can say it until you're blue in the face, but it's

not going to change the fact that I'm ready for another phase of my life."

"I'm not your next phase."

He grinned that dimpled grin, leaving a response up in the air.

Blowing out a breath, Donna decided that she needed some food in her stomach. But before she dug into her steak, she said, "I'm going to say this once and for all— I'm not ever going to settle down."

"Whatever you say, Donna."

As they ate, he didn't press the subject, and she felt herself relaxing little by little, even at the end of the evening, when he walked her out of the cabin to the porch.

"Thanks," she said, meaning it. This had been a great night. "You're a good host."

He left it at that, hovering over her, making her wonder if he was going to try to kiss her again.

Before he did, she started to walk. Fast.

"I'll take you back to the house," he said.

"I can make it on my own. Thanks, though."

As she made her way down the path from the cabin, she told herself not to look back, just as she'd done last night at the movie screening.

*Don't encourage him.*

*Don't...*

She did, stealing a glance over her shoulder. Then, in an effort to cover herself, she raised her hand in one last good-night to the handsome cowboy who'd put together such a beautiful candlelit night.

Just for her.


Caleb slept longer than usual since it was his day off, then took coffee at his leisure on the porch.

Last night's dinner had been a success as far as he was concerned. Donna hadn't looked at him as if he were a mutant from a parallel dimension—not even once—and she'd even opened up to him a little.

Or, at least, as much as a self-admitted ice queen might allow herself to do at this point.

He was slowly winning her over. He was sure of it.

The one moment he regretted was when he'd mentioned the fanciful—and somewhat screwy—notion of marrying into the Byrd family. He'd sure needed to ease his way out of that slip of the tongue. The last thing he wanted was for Donna to think that he'd wallowed around the ranch for years, dreaming of snagging a Byrd granddaughter just so he could officially be a part of their family. True, the idea was a nice one, but it didn't define him—or his attraction-at-first-sight to Donna.

There were just some things that were meant to be, he thought, and Donna Byrd was one of them.

After the coffee and a simple oatmeal breakfast, he took his truck off ranch, driving toward the Yellow Rose Estates, where Aunt Rosemary and Dad had taken up residence. He'd promised he would visit them once a week, and he hoped today would continue being the good day it'd started out to be…especially when it came to Dad.

When he pulled into the sunflower-lined driveway, he immediately spotted Aunt Rosemary on the porch, sitting in the swing. She was wearing white capris and sandals, along with a loose pink blouse that hid how skinny she'd been getting lately.

She saw him and stood up stiffly, as if her joints were tight. The overhead fan blew the sparse gray hair that was caught back in the plastic barrette she always wore.

Caleb waved, grabbing the bag of groceries he'd stopped to buy at the corner market, then getting out of the truck.

"How's your day going?" he asked as he came up the walkway that wound over the manicured lawn. Sprinklers were spraying water over the grass, huffing under the early-morning sun.

Rosemary smiled, but it was a polite, fixed one. "Today's not the best."

Caleb's heart sank. His visits always started with a "How's your day" and Aunt Rosemary's first reaction always set the tone.

He came up the steps, then enveloped her in a one-armed hug. She opened the door for him, leading him into an air-conditioned living room filled with knick-knacks she had collected from auction barns as well as the floral-patterned sofa and chairs Caleb had recently purchased for the house. The scent of potpourri rode over something medicinal that Caleb couldn't identify.

He found his dad in a recliner in front of the wide-screen TV, watching a baseball game. He wore gray slacks and an old white T-shirt with a dark stain over one side of his chest. His silver hair was wiry and stood straight up, as if he hadn't combed it yet.

"Hey, Dad," Caleb said. "Brought you some of those blueberry muffins you like."

"Shut up. I'm watching the game."

Yup, not a good day. No wonder Rosemary had been outside.

Caleb had learned this past year not to engage with his dad at times like this, so he continued into the kitchen. Rosemary followed him there.

"Caleb," she whispered in apology as she began unpacking the groceries, "yesterday he was fine. He was even telling me stories about some of those shows he watches. Ice truckers or some sort of thing. But this morning…"

Her voice faded while, in the family room, the volume of the TV rose. Sometimes any kind of noise—even the sound of refrigerators closing or bags rustling in the kitchen—could distract Dad from what he was concentrating on. He wanted to hear the game, not them.

"Don't worry, Rose." Caleb kissed her on the forehead and started walking with her toward the hallway, where they could talk without the din of the TV. "You doing okay?"

"We had a rough morning. He wanted to wear that darn shirt with the gravy stains that I've tried to throw away, but he always pitches a fit about it when he sees it's missing."

She clenched her hands by her sides, and Caleb could tell that there'd probably been some ugly words said. But she was as patient as a saint, and she'd promised herself that she would take care of her little brother through thick and thin years ago. He'd vowed the same, after their parents had died when they were younger.

"Choose your battles, right?" Caleb said, although it was occasionally impossible to do when Dad was on a roll and he said things that a person shouldn't have to endure. "Why don't you go somewhere fun today? See some friends, visit that tearoom you like."

Rosemary gave him a look—the "I don't think it's a good idea to leave you two alone" glance.

"I can deal with anything." Back when the dementia had first set in and Dad had refused to live with Caleb, he had done all the research he could about the malady—

and about keeping an eye on the primary caretaker, too. It was important that Aunt Rosemary get out of the house more than occasionally.

He scooted her toward her bedroom. "We'll have dinner together tonight when you get back, okay?"

She grabbed his hand. She had a strong grip, even though her skin was starting to look like worn, thin parchment.

"You're a good son," she said. "He's lucky to have you."

She kissed him on the cheek and went into her bedroom.

After she'd gotten her purse then gone, Caleb went back to the kitchen, eventually taking off his cowboy hat and hanging it on a rack by the back door. Then he fixed a snack for Dad—a muffin and iced tea—and brought it out to him on a tray.

He set it on a coffee table, near where Dad was propping his slippered feet.

Handing Dad the tea glass, he waited for the man to acknowledge him.

When he did, there was a muddled anger in his eyes, and Caleb felt an invisible punch to his gut.

"Your mom told you to get a damned haircut," Dad said. "You gonna defy her again?"

"I'll get it done."

"Useless idiot."

Caleb clenched his jaw and made sure his father had a grip on his tea. Then he sat on the nearby sofa. It was hard to even look at the once-vital man who had lost his power and his faculties. Knowing that it could happen to anyone scared the crap out of Caleb.

Even worse was the pent-up rage that roiled in him.

When most sons grew up, they had the chance to become closer to their fathers. But that opportunity had been taken away from Caleb.

More than ever, he had no idea who this man was from day to day.

As the baseball game loudly played on, Dad's eyes closed, and he drifted off to sleep. Caleb rescued the tea glass from the armrest where his father was loosely gripping it, then sat down again.

Maybe things would be different when Dad woke up. Maybe he would be lucid enough today to say something polite to Caleb; it'd happened a couple of times before.

Then again, maybe things wouldn't be different at all.

But if Tex were still here, he would've urged Caleb to keep on trying, no matter what. He would've reminded Caleb that the price of letting your family go without a fight was much too high.

As his father began to snore, Caleb liberated the TV remote and lowered the volume. There was still a chance that this would turn out to be a good day for Dad.

And a good day was all Caleb was asking for.

Donna would never admit to it, but since her dinner with Caleb, she'd been keeping her eye out for him.

And it wasn't because she was planning to sprint off in the other direction at the sight of him, either. Yesterday, which she'd known was his day off, she'd actually realized that she was hoping she would run into him by the fountain again, or maybe get another cocky text message telling her to check out the dream cabin.

But neither one had happened.

She told herself that was fine, though, because she was ever so busy with the same old stuff. Tracking her investments, keeping tabs on the state of the magazine industry, marketing the B and B and putting the finishing touches on the property, still checking in with their P.I. about Savannah and James to no avail....

Definitely busy.

Yet some kind of strange compulsion was making her yearn a bit for Caleb Granger, and it was confusing and very, very wrong. Hormones had been the downfall of so many—just look at her dad, Uncle William and Savannah for proof. But now, after she started to head toward some walking trails that she intended to design signage for, it was as if everything she'd learned about being independent and smart went by the wayside as she finally spotted Caleb's truck by the main house.

She slowed down without thinking, then watched how Caleb got out of his faded red vehicle to unload the last of the furniture that had been stored in a shed. As he grabbed an oak lamp stand that she had polished, bringing it up the steps of the main house, the muscles in his arms bulged, and she held her breath.

Muscles made by hard backbreaking work, she thought. Not the kind you got in a gym.

She was already halfway back to the house when she realized that she was traveling in the opposite direction than she'd first intended.

Caleb saw her as he came back out of the front door, and she braced herself for the dimples, for the overwhelming charm that had started to get the best of her.

But all she received from him was a tip of his hat.

"Morning, Donna," he said, then continued down the stairs toward his truck.

"Morning."

Would there be some banter now? Some teasing about how she had tracked *him* down this time?

Nope. He merely grabbed a small walnut magazine shelf and took it up the stairs.

Okay. She got it. Now that she'd had dinner with him, he was playing hard to get, challenging her to make the next move.

Well, good luck with that.

As he exited the house again, she noticed something about him. Even as he grinned at her, he seemed…distracted. He was still friendly, but he just wasn't the same Caleb.

Had something happened between their dinner and today?

"Caleb?" she asked as he walked past her.

His steps slowed, and he turned around.

"Is there…" Something going on?

He seemed to know what she was getting at, and he shrugged—his usual careless go-to gesture.

"It's just…" she said. "You seem preoccupied."

There. She'd left the door open for him to say one of his patently direct comments. *I'm already tired of you. The chase is over. Bored now.*

She could take anything he had to dish out.

It seemed as if he was about to say something, but then her damned phone rang.

One side of her wanted to check the number since she was waiting on so many calls. The other side wanted to hear what Caleb had to say, for whatever reason.

The side that told herself that caring was a bad idea finally glanced at the phone screen.

Unidentified number.

In the time it took for her to do that, Caleb was already on his way back to the truck. "I'll catch you later, Donna. They're waiting for me in the stables."

*Was* he playing hard to get?

As Caleb started his truck's engine, Donna realized that whoever had been trying to call her had gone to voice mail. She waited for them to leave a message while walking in the direction of the trails again, just to make it seem that she was as busy as Caleb, in case he was watching her in his rearview mirror.

When a blip of sound let her know that the caller had finished their message, she accessed it, telling herself not to look at Caleb as he drove off to wherever ladies' men went when they were done with a woman.

She came to a scuffing halt when she heard a female voice, traced with a dignified Texas drawl.

"Hi, Donna. I think you've been expecting my call."

An awkward pause—one just long enough so that Donna could hear her heart pounding in her ears.

"This is Savannah Carson. Or Savannah Jeffries. You would know that name better, I think."

Oh, God. This was happening.

Really happening.

The message continued. "Your P.I. contacted me a few times and…I've been trying to figure out how I was going to respond. I have to start off by saying that I'm not terribly surprised that I'm hearing from the Byrds. It's just been a long time since I…since I knew your father and uncle. I realized that somebody would get curious someday, but that doesn't mean I was prepared for this."

Another hesitation, and Donna crossed one arm over her chest, the other still holding the phone. Her pulse was drilling at her.

"Your P.I. explained everything—even that you all are aware of James. He's always known that I raised him as a single mom by choice, and he knows that his father has always been out of the picture. That he's in the world somewhere. But James doesn't know the entire story. It's not something I've ever been willing to share, and that's probably the reason…"

Savannah cut herself off. Had she almost said something about why she and her son were supposedly estranged?

"As I was saying," she said, her voice thick, "James is an adult, and I realized that I do owe it to him to tell him what I've learned from your investigator about your interest in us. I'm not sure how he'll respond to the possibility of meeting your family, though. And you should know that I'm not going to reveal to anyone who James's father is. There's been too much trouble about that already, and as long as you accept those terms, I'll go along with this."

As she paused again, Donna wondered, *What does she mean by "this"?* What was Savannah willing to go along with? Introducing herself to the family? Coming over for a fun-filled dinner with the Byrds with James in tow?

The woman ended by leaving her phone number, and Donna absently saved the message.

She wasn't sure how long she stood in the grass, with the roar of a Flying B truck in the distance and with the song of some birds blithely warbling nearby. But, eventually, she walked toward the dream cabin, dialing both Jenna and Tammy on the way so they could meet her in a place where there was no chance of anyone overhearing.

They'd been checking out the riding trails, so they

arrived at the cabin within fifteen minutes, tying their horses to a post at the side of the building and joining Donna on the porch, where the scent of honeysuckle massaged the air.

Donna played Savannah's message for them on speakerphone. When it was over, both Jenna and Tammy leaned back against the wall.

"Hot damn," Tammy said.

Jenna, who, like Tammy, was dressed in riding gear, asked, "So she's going to meet with us?"

"I'm not clear on that," Donna said. "I'll have to call her back to see. Not that I'm looking forward to it."

"We'll need to tell Aidan and Nathan about this," Jenna said.

"We can do that after we're done here. I just wanted to hear what you two thought first."

Tammy slid a hand to the back of her neck, under her dark ponytail. "What do you think James is going to say?"

"No use speculating," Donna said shortly. But then she thought better of it. Most of her life, she'd followed in her dad's footsteps, businesslike to the point of abruptness sometimes. Putting people at a distance.

But Tammy and Jenna deserved more.

They had to realize that she was just getting used to girl talk, because they both smiled patiently at her, waiting for her to go on.

"Sorry to be curt with you," she said. "This hasn't been the best week ever."

"Because of Savannah?" Tammy asked.

"Not just that." Donna told them about her financial advisor's email, too, but she skipped over Caleb's brush-off today.

That was something that shouldn't be affecting her at all.

Tammy came over to Donna, affectionately resting a hand on her shoulder. "Why're you worried about money when you already have a place to call home?"

Jenna flanked her other side. "You've got everything right here."

They meant well, and Donna tentatively reached out, touching her cousin's hand, then smiling at her sister. A warmth gathered around her heart, baking it.

Family, she thought. She really did have it.

She had almost everything except…

That emptiness that she often felt inside her seemed to expand, but she ignored it. She didn't even know what it was, not even when the image of Caleb's face flashed before her.

Jenna tilted her head. "You know what you need?"

A head examination? A winning ticket for the lottery?

Tammy was already grinning. "I know what you're going to say, Jen—half the staff is going for a night out, so we should go, too. After we talk to my brothers, we'll dance our cares away before we call Savannah in the morning. I have to say that Mike also needs to cut loose. He's been busier than usual this week, what, with all that flu going around Buckshot Hills."

Jenna linked arms with Donna. "I can hear Lone Star Lucy's calling us now."

Donna had never been to a honky-tonk in her life, but suddenly, a good time sounded like just the ticket.

"Why not?" she said, pausing, then drawing the women who'd become her best friends into a group hug.

A honky-tonk just might be as wonderful as the newest dance club or trendiest wine bar. She *would* dance her cares away there and maybe even meet someone who would temporarily take her mind off her problems.

Someone who wasn't named Caleb.

## Chapter Six

"Caleb," Hugh, the foreman, said at the end of the day as they sat at one of the staff's mess tables. "You really need a night out."

Caleb had been clearing his plate, and he looked down at the grizzled Hugh, who was just sitting there analyzing him like some kind of lifestyle coach, or whatever they called them.

He knew that Hugh had only addressed the subject now that they were the last ones to clear out tonight, seeing as a bunch of the other staff had planned to go to Lone Star Lucy's. It was Buckets of Beer night, and Caleb hadn't been to the honky-tonk since he'd gotten back from his leave of absence.

Hugh stood up with his plate, too. "You've looked about as blue as blue can be today, so I think a good time is in order. I could see that your dad did a number on you the minute you showed up to work this morning."

"I should be used to it by now."

"So what happened with him?"

"The usual." They walked alongside each other to the dish tubs, then deposited their tableware. "There're times I wonder whether it's the dementia that makes Dad say the things he does or if it's just because that's how he really feels about me and nothing's stopping him from telling me now."

"Don't let that stuff hound you. Forget about every bit of it. That's what honky-tonks are for."

The old man nudged his arm before he went his own way, to his cabin, where he never bothered with young men's nights out anymore himself.

But Caleb thought his friend might be right about letting loose with the rest of the staff....

As he walked to his cabin, he caught sight of the main house in the distance, and he wondered what Donna was doing tonight.

One thing was for sure—a woman like her wouldn't be at Lone Star Lucy's. And if ever she did happen to wander through the bar's doors, he doubted very highly that she would want to have a beer with him—not after he'd been so deep in his own problems this morning while trying to figure out just what he could do to make matters with his dad better.

He relived the moment when he'd seen her. Donna, with her blond hair and swerves and forever-long legs showcased by her sundress. But he'd been so distracted that he hadn't done the usual flirting, and it seemed that she'd taken his mood as a slight to her.

He hadn't even had the opportunity to tell her differently, because of his tight schedule and her ringing cell phone. Hell—she probably hadn't even thought about him once she'd gone about her business.

Turning away from the house, he went into his cabin. Maybe a night at Lucy's would make him forget about his ridiculous fascination with her. And maybe not.

As he spruced himself up, he kept thinking what she might make of the new cologne Aunt Rosemary had bought for him as a thank-you or the silver belt buckle he never got around to wearing.

So much for forgetting about Donna.

He decided against the cologne and the buckle, then hopped in his truck, zooming down the Flying B Road, his tires kicking up dust as he followed a few other vehicles that the staff were riding in.

It didn't take long to get to Lucy's, and once Caleb was inside the low-lit main room with its cramped tables and sawdust-covered floors, he ordered one beer, then settled in a chair next to Manny and his girlfriend, Maria.

"Small Town Saturday Night" was playing while Manny's cowboy hat rode his dark hair, his arm slung around Maria's shoulders.

"The man is *back!*" he said.

He clinked bottles with Caleb and they drank.

"So who's it gonna be tonight?" asked Manny.

Maria rolled her big brown eyes at the boy talk. "This is where I powder my nose. Excuse me, you two."

After Manny watched her go, he leaned his elbows on the scarred table and nodded toward the bar. "That cute redheaded vet is right over there, sneaking peeks at you. As I remember, she looked ready and willing to give you a thorough exam the last time we were here."

Caleb couldn't be less interested. He felt restless, as

if he didn't belong in places like this anymore. "I'm just here to kick back, Manny."

"Say it ain't so. Do you know how many good moves I've cribbed from you? Don't leave your student hanging."

"You've got Maria now, remember?"

"Who said I wasn't going to try everything I learn on her?"

Manny laughed and drank some more. Caleb couldn't help joining in with a chuckle, feeling a little more like himself as the songs changed from swinging numbers to two-stepping ballads.

Soon, Manny and Maria were on the floor, swaying to a Sugarland song, leaving Caleb to his own devices.

And that's when he looked up to see a stunning sight.

Donna Byrd, with her light hair shimmering around her shoulders, coming through the honky-tonk's door with her sister and cousin and their fiancés.

Caleb nearly did a double take, but after he gathered himself, he merely put his beer bottle on the table before he dropped it.

Donna. Here?

She sure as hell looked like a fish out of water, not necessarily because of the way she was dressed, but just because of the way she surveyed everything, as if each rustic chair and kitschy cowboy decoration on the walls might jump up and give her country cooties at any second.

Except for all that, she nearly blended in, wearing brand-spanking-new jeans and boots, plus a flirty cowgirl blouse that clung to every curve. But she was still straight from the city.

A fast Clay Walker song came on, and Caleb's heart

beat in time to the rhythm—skittering, banging, creating tightness in his belly.

A longing that built up the steam inside of him when all he'd meant to do tonight was work some of it off.

As Jenna and Tammy led Donna to a table in a corner, their fiancés, J.D. and Mike, went to the bar.

It was as if the room had gotten far more colorful and interesting with Donna in it, the music louder, the world less dull. It was like the first time Caleb had seen her all over again—chemistry and desire, wrapped into a searing bundle.

But there was something else, too, and once again Caleb wasn't sure what to name it. All he could do was want and need.

Manny had returned from the dance floor, leaving Maria across the room to chat with some of her friends near a stage where bands sometimes played. Unfortunately, Manny had seen where Caleb had been looking.

"Forget the redhead at the bar," he said. "Look who's here now."

Caleb shot him a don't-say-another-word glance, and Manny held up his hands.

"Sor-ry. It's no secret you have a thing for Donna Byrd, you know. Why don't you just go up to her and ask her to dance?" Then Manny chuckled. "Listen to me, giving the master tips."

Yeah, listen to him. Wasn't it strange that Caleb didn't know what to do with her?

Wasn't this a first?

Out of the corner of his eye, he saw Donna get up from her table and weave her way through a bunch of appreciative cowboys, over to the bar.

Before he could tell himself to stop watching her, he was standing, grabbing his half-full beer bottle.

"That's the man!" Manny said.

Caleb didn't react except to say, "I just need to fill the well, Manny. You want anything?"

"Yeah—a good view of what's about to happen."

Caleb narrowed his gaze at him before he left. So what if Manny was onto him? Wasn't everybody?

Wasn't Donna?

With each step he took toward her, his confidence grew. Everything his dad had said yesterday over dinner—about Caleb having as much value as a one-legged dog, about how much trouble he'd always caused him and Mom—seemed to dissipate as Caleb got closer to Donna.

Like Hugh said, he *could* forget.

She was at the end of the bar, where Doc Sanchez and J.D. were laughing with her. Caleb guessed it had something to do with the pink drink in the martini glass that she'd ordered in this land of beer and tequila.

J.D., whom Caleb had been working with in the stables lately, noticed him first.

"Caleb," he said, nodding in greeting.

Doc Mike smiled and raised one of the beer bottles from the bucket they'd purchased in a hello, too.

Donna slowly turned her gaze toward Caleb, her lips parted. In surprise?

But did he see a hint of a smile there before she corrected herself and went back to being blasé as she sipped her cocktail?

From their table, Jenna called to the men, and with knowing looks, they left Donna alone.

Just as Caleb thought she was about to follow them back to her group, he moved closer to her. "Wait a sec."

She lifted a cool eyebrow.

Great. It was obvious that his distance today on the ranch had pushed her back to square one, erasing any progress he'd made with that dream cabin dinner.

He didn't know if he should apologize or what, so he started out with a compliment. "You look real nice, Donna."

"These are my urban cowgirl clothes," she said. Then, as if she wanted to prove that she didn't give a crap about what he thought, she tossed back half her drink.

He chuckled. "What's in that glass?"

"It's called a Ruby. Grapefruit juice and vodka. In New York, there'd be sugared grapefruit slices as a garnish and maybe some sugar around the rim of the glass."

"We're not that fancy here."

"No kidding." She took another healthy swig.

If he hadn't known it before, he knew it now—she was definitely wielding some attitude.

"Listen," he said. "I didn't mean to be remote today when you said hi."

"You were? I didn't notice."

"Good."

She was so full of bull. It tickled him that she was pretending his attentions didn't matter. Mostly, the tickle got him in his chest, where, again, there was something more than lust happening with Donna. Something he hoped she *would* notice.

She finished off the drink, holding up a finger to the bartender to request a second.

"Another rough day?" he asked.

"Probably as tough as the one *you* were having earlier." She bit her lip, as if she was trying too late to hold back the words.

"Donna, I visited my dad yesterday. That's why I wasn't exactly Mr. Sunshine this morning."

As she pushed her finished cocktail away, she seemed sorry that she'd been giving him guff. "The visit didn't go well, I take it."

"Not so much."

She shifted her gaze to him and sighed. "Sorry for being difficult. Sorry for…I don't know. I think I'm sorry for everything lately."

Caleb didn't want her to be sorry.

Right then and there, he guaranteed that he would do anything he could to take away all the sorry from her.

The last thing Donna wanted to be tonight was a bummer, so after the bartender brought another drink, she motioned with her glass toward the back of the bar, where she'd seen pool tables.

"Care to join me in some game therapy?" she asked Caleb. It was as good as she could do for an olive branch.

He stepped back from the bar, indicating that she should lead the way.

As she passed him, she caught a whiff of his scent— a smell that belonged only to him. A smell that came to her at night sometimes, whether she wanted it or not.

The Ruby cocktail had given her a lift, so when they got to the back room, with some empty pool tables on one side and dartboards on the other, she put her drink down on a tall table. She went to a board and pulled out the darts.

"Are you safe to drink and dart?" Caleb asked with a grin.

"I'm fit as a fiddle." It was true. And she was also pretty relaxed, at that.

She proved it by moving into position away from the board and throwing a dart. She hit the nineteen point zone below the bull's-eye.

"Yee-haw," she said teasingly, then stepped aside for him to take a turn. "I strike first blood."

When Caleb took the dart from her, his index finger brushed hers. She didn't think he'd done it purposely, but even if he had, she wouldn't have felt a more powerful reaction.

A rumble deep inside.

A stirring that rocked her.

She realized that she'd held her breath, and as she forced herself to utilize oxygen like a normal person, she did her best not to look at him, to make eye contact and allow him to see what he'd done to her.

"What're you waiting for?" she asked instead, her tone challenging.

He shrugged, threw the dart, effortlessly hitting for twenty in the same kind of narrowed zone as she had, but for a point higher.

"Anything you can do," he said, grinning.

*I can do better.* She took his place, aiming with one eye shut, then nailing the green strip just outside the bull's-eye this time.

He waggled his eyebrows, his dimples at full force. "We could go on like this all night, or we could make this interesting."

*Danger, Donna Byrd,* said a little voice in her head. *Danger!*

But she was in a rather reckless mood. A Ruby-cocktail mood. She was tired of being beaten down by circumstances that she barely had control over. She was exhausted by attempting to stay even with the treadmill of problems that kept speeding under her.

"How interesting would you like to make this?" she asked.

He jerked his chin toward the board and, damn, it was sexy. Manly. The gesture tumbled her belly and tied it into knots of desire.

"If I hit the center," he said, "you will answer any question I ask."

"That's begging for trouble."

"I'll take it easy on you. Promise."

This time, when she crossed her arms over her chest, it wasn't a protective gesture. She was being just as cocky as he was.

"It's going to be fun to see you humbled," she said.

Wrong. Because he hit the bull's-eye with no problem.

Damn.

She spread her arms wide. "Okay. Have at it."

Her choice of words could've been better. Or maybe they were perfect, because a wicked gleam in his gaze told her that she'd hit her own bull's-eye in him.

Hah.

Caleb sauntered over to the board, plucking out the darts, then leaning against the wall. In his faded blue jeans, tattered boots, long-sleeved white shirt and that hat, he seemed like he should be out riding the range, not taking aim at her.

But when he did, his aim was true.

"What's the one thing I can do to persuade you to give me a chance, Donna Byrd?"

The directness of the question made the air snag in her lungs.

She'd only had one drink, and she was capable of holding a lot more liquor, but what she'd consumed had loosened her up enough so that she didn't mind answering.

Not this time.

"If I had the answer," she said, "I'd…"

"You'd tell me?"

Yes. Yes, she would, because tonight she'd informed Jenna and Tammy that she was going to dance and let go and have some fun. Maybe she would even do it with Caleb Granger because of that dinner they'd had together—an event that had broken some of the ice between them. Maybe she would do it because he'd so confidently bellied up to the bar and snapped her out of the funk that'd been caused by Savannah's phone message today.

Now, Donna took the biggest step she'd ever taken with a man—and it was in Caleb's direction.

As he saw her coming, that familiar heat took over his gaze.

But then, still in a teasing mood, she merely held out her hand for the darts.

He gave them over. "You're impossible."

"I try my best to be."

But she honored their bet, anyway, giving him a chance with her. Letting him in, just a little.

"You know why I came to this Lucy's place tonight?" she asked.

He seemed to know that she was giving him an opening. "Why?" he asked gently.

His voice. Why did it dismantle her?

"We got that call from Savannah today," she said.

He raised an eyebrow. "That's a good reason to need a drink."

"Tell me about it. She left a message, and I played it for Jenna and Tammy first. Then we had a chat with Nathan and Aidan before we came here, but we're going to wait until tomorrow to try to reach her."

"What did she say?"

"We think she really does want to meet us, even though she didn't come right out and say it. But she isn't sure how her son is going to react to everything."

"Understandably."

"She didn't sound happy about finally having to come clean with James about her past."

"She never told him?"

"It seems so." She shook her head. "After Tex asked her to leave the Flying B when he caught her and Dad together, she filed an incomplete at school, and neither Uncle William or Dad ever heard from her again. Neither of them tracked her down, either. There were hurt feelings all around, and I'm sure she didn't want James growing up knowing that there was a lot of pain involved with him."

Caleb furrowed his brow. "You sound pretty sympathetic to her."

"Maybe I am." Donna wasn't sure, but hearing Savannah's voice had made the woman more real than ever. "It's just…" *You can say it to him, Donna.* "It's just that I'm still so angry at Dad about this."

Even now, the anger was simmering in her. And, here, she'd thought that she'd put a lid on it for the time being.

She started to stick the darts back into the board, probably with more force than necessary. "Jenna made her peace with Dad, but I haven't yet. I used to think that man was the ultimate when I was growing up. I pushed back my anger about the divorce and what it did to my mom and tried to tell myself that he was my father, for heaven's sake, and he had to know much more about life than I did, so any decision he made had to be a decent one. But then we heard about Savannah…"

Caleb hadn't said a word. He just let her talk, then trail off, and she liked that about him. She'd never known many people who really knew how to listen like this.

She went on. "He's not the man I grew up admiring. He betrayed his own brother with a woman. Who does that?"

"I don't know."

"Jenna told me that he had his reasons, and even though she doesn't approve of what went down, she's forgiven him. I don't think I can."

"Maybe it'll just take some time."

"Maybe it'll never happen."

Caleb went quiet, and in the background, the country music played on, almost distant and blocked off by the walls of the dart room.

Finally, he spoke. "We never really know who they are."

His words didn't sink in at first. Perhaps Donna didn't want them to. But when they did, there was a profound ache that twisted in her.

He said, "We grow up thinking we know our parents, but then there comes a point when that changes. My situation's a little different than yours because my dad's literally someone I don't know on most days. But you had a rude awakening with yours. You never saw it coming."

She swallowed back the swelling in her throat. "He

*is* like an entirely different person now that this secret is out. And it's a hard thing to face."

At this moment, she'd never felt closer to anyone, even if she and Caleb were standing in a dim corner of a honky-tonk by a dartboard. Even if he was from a totally different world.

In spite of all her misgivings, she reached out with her free hand, touching a button on his shirt. But just as if it were made of fire, she let go.

What was she doing?

Her body knew, though, and it sizzled with the want of him…or of someone who understood her just as much as he did. And his body must've been doing the same thing, because as she was drawing back her hand, he clamped his fingers around her wrist.

"Don't," he said.

"What?" There was a clump of scratches in her throat that made her voice ragged.

"Don't draw back into that ice queen shell, Donna."

God, how she wanted to. It was safe in that shell. It was easy.

But as his fingers branded her, sending a trail of flame through her veins and then every other inch of her, she knew that the ice was melting.

Him, touching her. It felt so good, flaring her hormones so that every dark part of her lit up.

Donna finally raised her gaze, meeting his own. It was filled with such a fierce passion that she realized that she knew exactly what she needed tonight more than anything else.

She wanted them both to feel good, and she had no doubt that Caleb would know exactly how to accomplish that.

* * *

Fifteen minutes later, Caleb was still trying to wrap his mind around what had gone down with Donna inside Lone Star Lucy's.

One minute, they were playing darts. The next, Donna was making good on their bet and answering a question he'd never thought she would touch with a ten-foot pole.

And the next, her fingers had been on his shirt button, reaching out in a tentative gesture that had given him shattering pause.

She was *touching* him.

She was reaching out in a way he suspected that Donna didn't often do, if ever.

Even if his reputation might deny it, he would never take advantage of a raw moment for any woman. Caleb liked to play, but not if the board was tilted and he had an unfair advantage.

So he'd asked Donna if she needed to leave. She'd said yes, then said goodbye to her sister and cousin before getting into Caleb's truck.

And here they were, driving with her window down, the wind tangling her hair as she leaned back and closed her eyes. It wasn't until they reached the Flying B Road that she rolled up her window and looked at him straight on.

"Has anyone ever told you that you have a way about you, Caleb?"

He wasn't sure what the hell that meant. "A bad way?"

She laughed. "A good one. Believe it or not, I feel better than I did earlier tonight. It felt nice to spill my guts to someone who has another perspective."

He steered into the ranch, slowing down as they approached the main house.

As he came to a stop, she didn't make a move to get out.

"We're here," he said, as if she couldn't tell.

"It's still early. Don't you think it's still early?"

He gave her a curious glance. "Do you want to go *back* to Lucy's or something?" He wouldn't put it beyond her to change her mind.

"No. How about we drive around?"

All right, then. Without questioning her, he took off. When they were well on the road that traveled past the cabins, Donna pointed toward the east. "You can drop me off at the dream cabin."

"What?"

"I'm too hyped up on Ruby cocktails to go back to my room. But I have an idea. I'm going to lie down on that mattress. Why didn't I think of this before? I could have some sort of dream about how my family should handle everything with Savannah."

Maybe she *was* a lightweight who'd gotten drunk off of a little alcohol. "You know those stories about dreams coming true on that bed are just a heap of bull."

"No, they're not. Tammy had a so-called magical dream about Doc Mike on that bed that came true and vice versa. J.D. and Jenna, too."

"Are you sure you're not drunk?"

"Positive. You should see how many Rubys I've thrown down the hatch back in New York. Tonight was child's play."

Who was he to argue? He drove to the dream cabin, letting the engine idle.

Even then, Donna didn't get out. She merely unbuckled her seat belt.

"I guess I should wish you sweet dreams," he said.

She seemed at a loss as she toyed with the bottom of her blouse. But when she slipped him a look that he'd seen a hundred times from other women, he understood.

A "soft" look was what he would've called it.

Before he knew it, she'd slid closer to him, pushing back his hat and planting her other hand in his hair.

"Since the dart game," she said, "I've been waiting for you to kiss me."

Now it made sense, her touching his shirt button at the bar. It'd been Donna's way of starting things off between them.

But he'd thought it might take longer for her to come around. That it'd be a little more romantic. Was she reacting to all the stress she'd been under? Had tonight been her breaking point?

She tightened her hand in his hair, but he'd imagined a kiss like he'd never had with any other woman, not something fueled by whatever was egging her on.

"Donna," he whispered, stopping her.

Her gaze started to go cool as she released his hair.

"Donna," he said even more softly, cutting the engine, then easing his hand behind her neck, taking a moment to look into her eyes and to see the bewilderment there.

And the pure need.

Then, with all the time in the world, he kissed her right—his lips gently pressing against hers, fitting so perfectly as he tilted his head and rested his other hand under her jaw.

As he sipped at her, he rubbed his thumb against her neck, a slow cadence, promising so much more than the rushed encounter she'd been suggesting.

She moaned against his mouth, giving in, grabbing at his shirt as she went boneless against him. He tightened his grip on her, bringing her against him a little harder—but not too hard.

Just enough so he could deepen the kiss, opening his lips a bit more, demanding and asking all at the same time.

She answered by pulling him toward her and leaning back so that her spine was flush against the seat, her light hair spilling over the vinyl.

"Caleb," she whispered.

The sound of his name coming from Donna Byrd was like sparks coming into contact with oil.

And, suddenly, Caleb wasn't sure how he could hold back anymore with the woman he was crazy about.

## Chapter Seven

*Just one time with him,* Donna thought as a bolt of desire split her straight down to the piercing ache between her legs.

She needed Caleb tonight, and there didn't have to be more to this than anything physical. After all, she was going to be leaving this ranch as soon as the B and B opened and she could run the marketing program from miles away.

Their differences wouldn't matter if he kept on kissing her like this, his lips nestled just under her ear and sending brutal shivers through her, making her lift her hips against his. They were just two people who wanted the same thing.

Each other.

Desire seared her from the inside out as he dragged his lips to the center of her neck. She knocked his hat all the way off, and it hit the floorboards as she threaded her fingers through his shaggy blond hair.

"You do know how to kiss," she said on a thin breath.

He ran his mouth up to her jaw, skimming over it, his body pressing the wind out of her as he lay half on top of her. His muscled length felt so good, a fit that allowed her to wiggle her hips and encourage him.

She felt his excitement through his jeans, and that urged her to reach a hand between them, grasping for the buttons on his fly.

That emptiness she'd been feeling for a while now... she needed to fill it, and this was how she would accomplish that mission. It was the only solution she knew.

"Whoa, Donna," he said, rising up just enough to look down at her. "Not so fast."

His eyes were so blue. "You're usually faster than I am."

"Not tonight."

He leaned on his forearms, slowing everything down except for her wild heartbeat. And when he gazed at her, using his fingertips to coax her hair back from her face as if all he wanted to do was memorize her, something scary and silly rotated in her belly, flipping it and sending another zing of passion to the juncture of her thighs.

"What do you mean you're not fast tonight?" she asked.

"I mean that this isn't going to be wham-bam-and-thank-you-ma'am."

He eased his mouth to her temple, kissing her there. She closed her eyes, her pulse suspending.

"What I mean," he said, leisurely kissing her lower, near the tip of her mouth, "is that we're going to take our sweet time together."

Another twist of need got her where it counted, making her want him all the more, especially when he kissed her full on the mouth again.

His lips were softer than she ever could've anticipated and, for a second, taking things slow seemed the best idea in the world.

Slow kisses, slow fingers unbuttoning her blouse, slow anticipation as he parted the material.

Her chest heaved, her breasts pushing against the lace of her bra. The moonlight coming through the windshield showed his expression of sheer, ragged appetite as he ran a gaze over her.

When Caleb tenderly slid his hands under her back and returned to kissing her, long and sultry and adoring enough to rip her apart, she made a tiny sound of delight under his mouth. She hadn't expected another kiss, just groping.

Just wham-bam, because that's all she'd ever really had before.

Languidly, he drew on her mouth, then used his tongue to prolong the kiss, to taste her, to explore so much of her that she couldn't stop herself from arching against him, making him moan.

The primal sound put her back in a safe mental place, because it reassured her that he also wanted what she'd come here for—they wouldn't need emotions, just action. She'd known just what she was doing when she'd asked him to bring her to the dream cabin. It wasn't as if she could suggest that he come to her room in the main house, and she didn't love the idea of the other ranch hands catching them sneaking into his place.

When he kissed down her chin, her neck, then to the

tops of her breasts, she pressed her hand against the back of his head, enticing him to go on.

"Front clasp," she whispered. She was talking about her bra.

He reached up, and with no fumbling at all, undid it.

As her breasts were freed, she felt the night air on them, felt his lips as he covered every inch, using his hands to shape her, too.

She reached over her head, grasping for the door. She needed to hold on to something because his mouth was taking her for a ride—he was sucking at her now, his fingers pleasuring her other nipple until both of her tips stood at stiff peaks.

So sensitive there. So…

She hauled in a breath, sharp and surprised, as he used his tongue to work her into an even more demanding frenzy.

"Come on," she said, nearly pulling at his hair again. "Almost—"

As a crashing bang shot through her, she bucked, the sensation reverberating through every cell with violent echoes. She thought she heard herself cry out, but she wasn't sure—not as Caleb gnawed his way down her stomach, toward her belly.

Just as she became a squirming mess again, he slowed down even more, then halted altogether.

"What is it?" she asked.

"I just realized," he said against her skin, looking up at her with that devilish gaze and that dimpled smile. "We've got a feather bed waiting for us."

She'd intended to get there at some point—but the sooner the better now.

He whisked her into his arms, and before she knew

it, he'd barged out the truck door and was carrying her up the porch steps.

When they entered the cabin's door, it was with another crash. Immediately, she pushed herself out of his arms until she was standing, pulling at his shirt, leading him across the floor of the one-room cabin with his lips against hers, kissing feverishly.

They bumped into a chair, banged into a table. She didn't know where the hell they were going—she just hoped they somehow made it to the bed before they both exploded.

When he lifted her up, onto the table—in the kitchen area?—she forgot the bed altogether.

He was already stripping off his shirt, and she did the same with hers, tossing that and her bra to the floor, then taking care of her boots and socks, too. She tore at the fly of her jeans.

But his hand halted her.

"Let me," he said.

Her chest was rising and falling as she gave him all the control he'd asked for, as she leaned back and braced her hands on the table's surface.

He rested his palms on her thighs as she pulsed with ravenous hunger. Then, with deliberate care, he brought his hands upward, until one of them reached the middle of her legs.

As he rubbed her there, she almost fell backward onto the table, but he made sure she didn't by bringing his other arm around her back, holding her up.

"Is my technique modern enough for you?" he asked, grit in his tone.

"You'll…" She gathered her breath. "You'll have to give me more of a demonstration."

He laughed, low and sexy, traveling his fingers to her zipper. As he undid it, the sound filled the room, eating its way through her, too.

He coasted his fingers into her open fly, into her panties, spreading her legs wider.

"Does that help you reach a conclusion?" he asked.

"It will."

Donna could feel him watching her face, and something told her to make him wait for a so-called conclusion, to put him through as much as he was putting her through before she rewarded him with a climactic reaction.

"Even so," she said, barely getting the words out, "you're making great progress."

He stroked her thoroughly with his fingers, up and down, his thumb circling her most private spot just before he slipped inside of her.

She couldn't take anymore, and she lost all strength, falling into his arm, which had been supporting her this entire time.

With a guttural sound that told her he'd almost reached a breaking point himself, he scooped her into his arms again, then laid her down on the feather bed.

It was soft against her back as they sank into it, as he guided the jeans from her body, then her panties, leaving her fully exposed to him in the moonlight coming through the nearest window.

More exposed than she wanted to admit, because her heart felt tight in her chest, as if it didn't know which way to go now.

He left the bed, and she heard him doffing his jeans and the rest of his clothes, then returning to her.

As he came body to body with her again, she bit her

lip. His flesh against hers. When had it ever felt this wonderful?

*Why* was it feeling this wonderful when all it should be was a casual encounter?

He'd put on a condom, and the tip of him nudged her, teasing her.

She realized she'd never needed anything more in her life than what she needed now—him inside of her. Caleb Granger, the man she'd thought was wrong in every way.

When he entered her, she held her breath. He traveled deep, but she took him all in, moving with him, holding one of his hands as they churned, hips to hips, her to him.

She imagined water, her favorite fountain in Central Park, then the one outside of the Byrds' main house. The rhythm started slow, lazy, but then began to rush through her, flooding her with feeling, gathering into a wall of emotion that threatened to crash down on her.

But even though Donna would've run away from sensations like this before tonight, she felt herself opening to this man, waiting for the crescendo she could feel building inside of her, and of him.

And when it finally pummeled her, it got her with a crushing smash, once, twice—

As she stiffened at the third incredible assault, she let out all the breath she had, coming down from her high, her legs wrapped around him so tightly that they were pretty much one person. He had climaxed before her and had his mouth pressed to her neck, his lips formed into the silent shape of her name.

As their breathing evened out, she didn't let go of him.

Not yet.

* * *

Caleb moved his lips to Donna's in the aftermath—a sweaty, no-holds-barred, postorgasm kiss—and, after they drew away from each other and looked into each other's gazes, he half expected her to tell him this was it.

*Impressive,* she might say, suddenly cool, then hopping out of bed to hurriedly get back into her clothes. *Glad we made it to the bed, at least.*

But she wasn't going anywhere, instead curling into his chest.

He reveled in the intimacy, cradling her as she pulled him even closer with one of her legs, which was wrapped over his hip. He was still inside of her.

Near silence reigned—the still of a country night, the thud of his heartbeat slowing down from all the excitement. He drew circles on her lower back. He loved feeling the swell of her rear end just below his fingers, loved how curvy she was.

Loved…

Just about everything about her?

Or was this still an attraction at first sight?

"That was…" she started to say.

"How about we don't talk just yet." He didn't want to know what she was going to say to work her way out of bed and through the door.

"I want to tell you that I'm glad you kept pursuing me, Caleb. Tonight was worth it."

He laughed softly into her hair. The sweet lemony scent of it filled him.

They lay there like that for a bit, quiet and satisfied, but he knew he'd have to move soon, clean up, then come back to bed where she would hopefully be waiting.

Yet, when she slipped her hand between them and

touched his belly, trailing a finger along the line of hair that brushed down to his groin, he wondered if he knew anything about where this was going at all.

"What're you doing, Donna?" he asked.

In answer, she lifted her face to kiss him, and it wasn't long until he was getting revved up again.

What was he—seventeen?

Without doing much thinking—yup, just like the seventeen-year-old he used to be—he told her to wait. Then he discarded the rubber, barely even looking at it because he just wanted to be back in bed again.

They made out like starved kids on homecoming night, exploring more of each other's bodies, laughing, clinging, coming to completion until they were both exhausted.

This time, as he held her, he closed his eyes.

"Men," Donna said, laughing. "Who's the weaker species—the women who can stay awake after some exertion or the guys who don't have an ounce of gas left?"

"No debating," he said, his voice already fading.

"Okay."

From the pressure on the mattress, he could tell that she was shifting her weight, and he opened one eye to see her leaning on an elbow, propping herself up to look at him. They'd gotten under the sheets somehow, but he could see the swell of her breasts above them.

He smiled, closing his eyes again.

"So how many girlfriends have you had?" she asked.

Oh, brother. "Don't know."

"Yes, you do. You just don't want to tell me."

"Not as many as you think."

"That's okay. A gentleman never tells, right? And that means I don't have to talk about my past, either."

He felt the tip of her finger running down his nose. It gladdened his heart and gave him a tingle, and he forced open one eye again to gauge her.

But then the reality of what she'd said hit him: She didn't want to tell him about ex-boyfriends because that's what people did with each other only if they planned on having more than a one-night stand.

Donna must've read the look on his face, because her voice lowered to a more tender tone than he'd ever heard from her.

An afterglow voice.

"You've got that expression, Caleb, like you're expecting something from me."

He really didn't want to talk about this now, and he put his hand on her hip, hoping she would understand what he was saying without him having to say it. Hoping that they could save this conversation for later.

She leaned over, kissing his forehead, then whispered against his skin.

"I meant what I said about your giving me a great night."

But he was already going to sleep, thinking that there'd be time enough in the future to persuade her that there was much more to come for them.

After all, hadn't she already been persuaded this far?

He looked so sweet when he slept, Donna thought as she watched the moonlight comb over Caleb. It was only now, when he couldn't see her that she felt free to think such things, to look at him as much as she wanted and to smile as she did it.

Her skin—and everything under it—was still singing. And, once again, that danger signal lit through her, telling her to watch it—that there was a possibility that she might get addicted to him.

That she might never want to leave the Flying B.

But she was sure that, once morning came, she'd be back to normal, wanting the same things she'd always wanted, never deviating, always focusing like a laser on success and security.

And Caleb wasn't secure. No one was.

Donna had always depended on herself and it'd worked out pretty well so far.

She lay down, closing her eyes and listening to the cadence of his breathing, realizing that she was matching it with her own. She tried not to acknowledge that lonely gaping spot already reopening in her, because she was merely emotional right now. Swept away by hormones.

It would pass. She'd never felt this much before, but she was sure it would go away.

Soon she was floating toward sleep, her mind cartwheeling with vivid memories of tonight—Lone Star Lucy's, kissing in Caleb's truck, the feel of his hands and mouth all over her.

Plus even more than that.

She was only faintly aware of the new images, though—strange ones that wove in and out of reality: An open blue sky above her, stretching forever in all directions. The scent of grass, the feel of a blanket beneath her back.

She had one hand tucked under her head, and she was wearing a loose flannel dress with long sleeves and cowboy boots. A country dress. Around her, birds sang and, in the near distance, she could hear...

Laughter?

Lots of it. And she was one of the people laughing,

but it was to herself, because she had her other hand cupped over her belly and—

Donna woke up with a start. A trickle of sweat was winding its way between her bare breasts, the sheet dipping to her waist as she pressed her hand to her stomach.

Had she been dreaming that her tummy was curved, as if she were…

Pregnant?

It all came back to her now—the nightmare, the course of events that had gotten her here, in a feather bed where so many others had had dreams that came true.

Most of all, though, she realized that Caleb Granger was lying stomach-down next to her, the emerging sunlight streaming through the window, making his skin golden as it stretched over the muscles of his back and arms.

For a stray, happy moment, her heart reached out to him, remembering last night. But it wasn't her heart that'd been touched by him, right? He'd done a good job with the rest of her.

He was never going to get to her heart.

As she tried to make sense of everything, panic set in. That dream…

A baby?

No way. Because how would one of those fit into her life?

How would the father of that baby fit?

Right, there was just no way. There was no future.

Attempting to be as silent as a ninja, she slipped out from under the sheets. One of her feet hit the floor, and she was just about to touch down with the other when she heard Caleb moving.

Dammit.

She took a peek over her shoulder, but he had merely stretched out an arm, as if he'd wanted to feel her body next to his.

Okay. She could get out of here before he woke up. She'd already heavily hinted for him not to expect anything beyond one night, so was there really any reason to say goodbye before she left?

Yup, because after she slipped out of bed all the way and was putting on her jeans, she saw him sleepily running his hand over the indentation where she'd been.

Then he opened his eyes.

Donna almost folded her arms over her naked breasts, then thought better of it, quickly jerking her bra off the floor and shrugging into it.

Caleb got one of those arrogant grins on his face and leaned his head on his palm. "Don't tell me—you turn back into a pumpkin at the crack of dawn."

"You need to start work soon, don't you?"

She snatched her blouse off the floor, her pulse going a mile a minute as she pulled the material over her, fumbling with the buttons until she made herself slow down.

"Funny," he said. "It's almost as if you were trying to sneak out of here before I woke up."

Damn, she couldn't take her eyes off his chest and the corrugated abs that disappeared beneath the sheet. She managed to deprive herself, though.

"I thought I'd let you sleep a little longer," she said. "No use bothering you."

"Donna."

All right—there wasn't an excuse in the world that would get her out of this.

She would button the rest of her blouse later. "Caleb.

This wasn't meant to be something that was going to last a lifetime. I thought you knew that."

"You've been clear about a lot of things, but somehow, a lot of your convictions disappeared last night. Why wouldn't you change your mind about other matters, too?"

"I was caught up in a moment."

"And you could have a lot more of those moments with me."

Good heavens. He just never gave up. Unfortunately, she'd given him good reason not to.

Her shoulders sank a bit. She didn't want to be cruel, but she didn't want to raise his hopes for the long run, either. She'd never promised anything but one night.

"No matter how good the sex was," she said, "this isn't going to happen again."

"Pardon me for saying so, but your body language speaks volumes more than what comes out of your mouth."

She frowned at him as he sat up in bed, not seeming to care that the sheet bunched just below his belly. It was a move that shouted his confidence about her giving in to more than she'd ever bargained for.

"Last night," she said, "was an aberration. I was emotional and, hence, willing."

He nodded, as if he was merely hearing her out until she came to her senses.

"I mean it," she said. "Good sex isn't enough to keep me on the Flying B forever."

"It was more than good sex, and you know it."

Her mouth hung open with a retort that never came. That's because she suspected he might be right.

But he couldn't be. She hadn't fallen for him as he'd

supposedly done for her already. Plus, the Flying B wasn't who she was or what she was meant to do.

She decided to try a different tack with him. "Even if I wanted to stay here, I've got way too much going on to have some kind of relationship with you."

"You mean distractions like Savannah, James, all that."

Caleb lay back and tucked a hand behind his head, just as she'd been doing in that dream. It was unnerving.

"The thing is, Donna," he said lethargically, "you seem to like it when I understand your troubles. Admit it—I'm probably the only man who's ever really gotten you."

He was making way too many good points.

"I'll admit you're a great listener," she said. "And I feel much better now, after last night."

"Sexual healing, huh?"

He had the grin of a man who recognized a desperate woman's justifications, and it was frightening her to death. Because what could you say to a guy like that?

How could you convince him that he was wrong?

She didn't even take the time to put on her socks and boots, because she had to get out of here before he worked his wiles on her again, making her think it was a good idea to give in to every heated whim that had started to attack her at the sight of his skin.

What had she been thinking, giving him an inch when she knew he'd take a mile?

"I've got to go," she said, her hand on the doorknob.

"See you soon."

She huffed out an exasperated sigh, but once she'd exited and gone down the steps, her libido began to take up where Caleb's arguments had left off.

*You'll see him again, all right.*
*And you'll like it.*

She began walking away, bare feet and all, before her confused heart could chime in, too.

## Chapter Eight

Caleb realized something important after Donna left and he cleaned up the dream cabin, then drove back to his own place to get ready for the day's work.

Donna, who'd always moved so fast in the city, really *did* need a slow touch when it came to matters of the heart.

But if she and he had gone a little too quickly last night, he certainly didn't regret it. Nope, he firmly believed that what he needed to do now was persuade her that it wasn't just sex that she wanted.

He wouldn't even let it bother him that she had taken off like a shot as soon as dawn had hit the sky.

Actually, that did bug him a little. She'd been jumpy as hell, as if… Had she dreamed in that feather bed last night, just like in all the family legends?

Nah. He didn't want to jump to conclusions. After all, Caleb himself had slept like a rock, so he still didn't believe all those magical tales. He didn't need any supposedly charmed mattress to give him dreams when he already knew what they were: to make Donna Byrd see that he was the one for her.

And he stuck to that theory as he arrived at the stables, where Hugh asked Caleb to deviate in his regular schedule for the time being. The foreman left J.D. with the horses—a job that had belonged to Caleb for about fifteen years now—and had Caleb work only on the cattle side of the operation today, just as he'd done back when he'd been new on the ranch.

No horses. No setting his own schedule.

Hugh didn't explain his reasons while he performed maintenance on ditches and pipes with the hands until lunch, and Caleb didn't ask.

At the midday meal, he ran into J.D. in line for the pork chops, potatoes and grilled vegetables.

Caleb greeted Jenna's fiancé, then said, "If I didn't know better, I'd say Hugh's giving my old job to you. I was always the horse guy around here."

"I heard you grew up doing a little of everything on this ranch. You started out with the cattle, right?"

"Until Tex asked me to personally maintain his stables. I know we've added to them lately, but..."

J.D. smiled. "You don't think that Hugh's getting ready to retire soon and he's gearing up to groom you as the foreman?"

It'd occurred to Caleb, but he didn't want that to happen sooner rather than later. "Hugh's got a lot of good years left in him."

"Who knows?" As they sat at a bench, J.D. nudged back his hat, revealing some of his short, dark hair. "Change is in the air here, and not just with Hugh. There also seems to be a lot of pheromones floating around the Flying B lately and throwing a lot of curves to the personnel."

From the teasing glint in his brown eyes, he was referring to last night and how Caleb had driven Donna home from Lone Star Lucy's.

Caleb sat down, too. "I think I should be pretending that I have no idea what you're talking about."

"Is that what Donna wants? Secrecy?"

Caleb grinned. "Donna who?"

They laughed.

"You can pretend all you want, Caleb, but there isn't a person here who doesn't know better."

They dug into their food. J.D. wasn't kidding—everyone probably knew that he'd driven Donna home last night. What happened afterward was up to anyone's imagination, but Caleb was a realistic man.

And he wasn't into hiding how he felt about this woman.

Labor ended at dusk. Since he was used to hard work in the stables, anyway, Caleb had a quick dinner in his kitchen then got ready to go out. But this time he didn't put on a fancy suit or slick back his hair, and he wasn't preparing to make his way to a honky-tonk.

He was going to be his very own kind of subtle with Donna tonight.

By the time he drove up to the main house, night had fully embraced the sky. He parked under the window he knew belonged to Donna's room. The light was on, so he gambled that she was in there, working.

Taking out his phone, he sent her a text.

Take a look outside, Donna Byrd.

While he waited, he removed his hat and held it in his hands. His pulse was skittering, just like some kid was throwing stones over the surface of a pond.

Was he really ready for this—a relationship with Donna?

As he stood there, he realized that she really hadn't just been something different that had caught his eye and his fancy. He had sincerely lost his heart to her on day one.

It didn't take but a minute for the window to open and for Donna to lean out. She was wearing a simple yellow sleeveless blouse, her blond hair tied back.

Were her eyes shining as she looked down at him?

"Caleb…" she said with a warning tone.

Maybe not. "Sorry for resorting to a text message, but I chose that instead of tossing pebbles at your window. It's a more modern way of communicating, you see."

"I thought I told you—"

"That I should stop by tonight to give you a break from work?"

As he flashed his best smile, she rolled her eyes, but she didn't shut the window on him. Surely *that* was a good sign.

"Take a break, Donna," he said. "There's some country culture I want you to partake of before you go back to your hors d'oeuvres in the city."

She lowered her head as she leaned on the windowsill, and he knew that he was breaking her down, minute by minute, night by night.

"Donna," he said softly. "I'm not here with the hopes that tonight's going to end up like last night. Consider my intentions pure."

"Pure baloney," she muttered with her face still lowered, but it was loud enough for him to catch it.

He laughed. "Have you ever had a fried Oreo?"

She peered up. One thing Caleb knew was that women and sugar went well together. He was hoping the same would hold true in Donna's case, and it would serve as an excuse for her to come out with him tonight, even for a short time.

"They've got them at the high school," he said. "The PTA is putting on their usual summer festival to raise money. One of the booths has deep-fried everything, and the Glee Club moms make homemade vanilla ice cream to go with the Oreos. They say it's a Buckshot Hills tradition."

She finally stood, then sat on the windowsill. The sheer curtains flirted with her bare arm.

"Couldn't you just bring me back a few?" she asked.

"They're no good if they're not fresh. At least, that's my expert opinion."

"I don't think fresh is a big selling point with a so-called 'food' that's preserved to within an inch of its life." She slid a glance to him.

She needed just a tiny nudge more. "It's only a fifteen-minute drive," he said.

"It's not the travel time that's making me hesitate."

There it was. Caleb wasn't going to get anywhere with her until they faced the fallout from last night.

"Just come down here, Donna," he said, his tone determined. "Oreos or not, we've got a thing or two to straighten out."

She paused, shrugged, then shut the window.

Shoving his hat back onto his head, he meandered

over to the passenger side of his truck, hoping she'd just climb inside for a ride without giving him much grief.

Sure enough, she came out of the back of the main house, looking so gorgeous in that yellow shirt, a short jean skirt and sandals, that he couldn't take his gaze off her.

But he managed, just so she would see that he was serious about a talk.

She went for the door handle, then got into the truck before he could hold the door open for her. His blood surged at the citrus scent of her.

"Let's go get some of those heart attacks waiting to happen," she said, looking out of the windshield, as cool as ever.

But she had a flush on her cheeks, as if she was recalling last night.

In an optimistic mood, he went to his side of the truck, starting up the engine, well on his way to where he ultimately intended to go with Donna.

Donna had never known that she could be just as impulsive as Caleb was.

If anyone had asked her what she would be doing tonight, she wouldn't have answered, "Oh, I'll be on a joyride with the guy I burned rubber away from this morning. And I'll have no earthly idea why I said yes to taking off with him when I knew better."

She kept telling herself that they really did need to talk this out. If anything, it wasn't a bad idea to stay friendly with Caleb, because who needed drama between them when there was enough of that going around, anyway?

But clearly, the fact that he'd shown up at her window

tonight like a thickheaded Romeo told her that nothing she'd said this morning had sunk into that noggin of his.

So why had her heart given a bunny leap when she'd seen his cell phone text? And why had she rushed to the window like a misguided Juliet before she'd gotten ahold of herself and calmly opened it?

Because she'd been thinking about him the entire day, she thought. Because she *was* addicted, just as she'd feared she would be. Addicted to the memory of bodies rubbing against each other. Addicted to an overwhelming rush she'd never experienced before.

Yes, it was a good idea to talk to him and put a stop to his nonsense once and for all, and an Oreo run was as good a time to do it as any.

They were on the Flying B Road going away from the ranch when he asked, "What's got you holed up in that room tonight?"

"Wild guess." She protected her emotions, because it was family talk that had gotten her into the position—or, rather, the *positions*—she'd found herself in last night with him.

"You returned Savannah's call?" he asked.

"You've got it." In her peripheral vision, she saw how he casually rested his hand on the steering wheel and mildly slumped in his seat—sexy and careless. She blew out a breath. "Everyone in the family got together this morning and made the call together. Savannah wasn't available, so we left a message. I'll admit, though, that I was just waiting around in my room tonight, doing busywork and hoping she'd call back."

"What if she still does?"

"I've got my phone with me. But it could take days

for her to get back to us, just like before, when our P.I. contacted her."

Caleb smelled so good, damn him. Donna got as close to the door as she could, but it was still as if he were on her skin, sending shivers over it, caressing it.

"It could be," he said, "that Savannah's trying to talk James into the answer most of the Byrds want to hear."

"What—that he'll meet with us? I have to say that there's a cowardly side of me that wouldn't mind if he avoided us for the rest of his life. But the other side of me has gotten too curious about him and Savannah, and I don't know if I'll ever be able to let it go if they don't materialize."

And…here she was again, talking to Caleb as if he were her best friend in the world.

It was as if it'd happened so quickly that she hadn't seen it coming, but it'd started to feel as natural as…

As water flowing, carrying itself from one place to another.

Why not truly be Caleb's friend? Wouldn't that be good enough, now that they'd gotten the chemical attraction out of their systems?

"Uncle William and Dad are coming back to the Flying B this weekend," she said. "You probably heard that I planned a party to make the staff officially at home for the B and B, even though we aren't having our grand opening for about a month and a half. Dad said they'd be there for it."

"Is it time for you to hash things out with Sam?"

Hearing him say it out loud made her stomach bunch up. "I won't be able to avoid him, as much as I'd like to."

Caleb got quiet as they turned onto a road that led toward town, ghostly white fences whooshing by.

Finally, he said, "If you have the chance to make things right, Donna, take it. You never know when it'll be too late."

He was talking about *his* dad, and she felt petty. Because he was right.

"Are there ever times when you believe your father is thinking clearly?" she asked. "When his mind is strong enough so that you can have the same kind of conversation with him that I need to have with my dad?"

"There're moments. Few and far between. But I can't catch all of them because when I'm around him, he usually gets worse. And that's bad for Aunt Rosemary."

"God, Caleb."

"It is what it is." But she could tell that it still disturbed him.

They didn't say much else until they reached the high school, which consisted of a large brick building that stood across a parking lot from a matching structure— the combined grade and middle school.

After they parked, he went around to her side and opened her door, standing aside to let her pass. He was giving her room tonight, and she almost missed the more persistent Caleb.

Almost.

The festival was in a field at the back of the high school, where there was a simple sign that read, Fairgrounds. A small Ferris wheel lit up the night, and there was a Tilt-a-Whirl, Scrambler and Round Up completing the ride selections. Basically, there were booths featuring student-run midway games, snacks, homemade goodies like jams and quilts, plus campus clubs that were getting a head start on the school year.

The unmistakable aroma of deep-fried fat snaked to

her as they passed a bunch of kids out on a summer's night. It was too late for families, it seemed, and some of the booths were even beginning to close up shop.

"Is this the place to be in Buckshot Hills right now?" she asked.

"For the few nights that the PTA puts this festival on."

"What does everyone do when there's not a festival?"

"Mostly, the families hang out at their homes during the summer. Kids still play on their neighborhood streets and come in when the lights turn on. The teenagers cruise by the bowling alley and sometimes go to the movies and the local hamburger joint."

Donna would've screamed with boredom if she'd grown up here, but there was something very homey about the knowledge that there was still a place where kids would rather run around outside with their friends instead of staying inside to play video games.

They came to the deep-fried booth, where a whip-thin woman in a Glee Club apron was managing orders while a few more took care of the cooking—blending the batter, dipping the cookies into it, then sinking the Oreos into pots of oil.

The apron woman gave two already-prepared plates to Donna and Caleb when it was their turn in line. The cookies were sprinkled with powdered sugar, and there was a mound of vanilla ice cream on the side.

They walked toward a picnic bench away from everyone else. In the background, rock and roll played from the Ferris wheel.

"Well," she said, sitting down. "Thanks for killing me slowly."

"Enjoy." He grinned, then dipped his Oreo in the

ice cream and took a big bite, leaving powdered sugar around his mouth.

Really? Did she *have* to sit here and die to wipe that sugar off him?

Or, worse yet, to kiss it off?

She concentrated on her own snack, using the napkin efficiently so she wouldn't give him any powdered-sugar ideas.

He gestured toward the Tilt-A-Whirl. "Fair warning—I just saw a couple of ranch hands who work with our cattle over there. We could leave if—"

"I'm not embarrassed to be seen with you." She put her cookie down. She was already full, even after a couple of bites. "I merely don't want anyone to get the wrong impression about us."

"People aren't blind, Donna."

"I know. I wasn't exactly discreet last night." She'd never had an undercover affair in her life, so why did she feel as if she couldn't flaunt Caleb here and now?

Was there something she wanted to keep intimate? Something that *mattered* with him?

She shook off the very idea. "In a couple months, you're going to laugh about your romantic ideas or this… whatever it is you have for me. It's all going to wear off by then and you'll have moved on."

"How do you know that?"

His gaze was that steady light blue that always swayed her.

"We discussed this," she said, her voice hoarse. She cleared her throat. "You've been working off of a fantasy. Last night was just an extension of it, because I was in that cabin for one thing, and I think you were in it for another."

He pushed away his empty plate, and what he said next jarred her more than anything he'd ever said before.

"I'm fully aware I created a fantasy at first, but now it's the real thing, Donna. And I'm not going to give up on something I know is so right."

She knew her eyes had never been so wide, her gaze never so confused, and she didn't want him to see that in her.

So she cooled, just as she always did. "I'm only trying to save you the trouble."

And she meant it, as she got up from the bench and walked back to the truck.

She'd failed at her magazine business and failed in her finances. He didn't need to be included in that list.

Even the next day, Caleb's confession rang through Donna.

And that was why she finally called her first ever silly girl talk meeting off the ranch at the Longbranch Diner.

She, Tammy and Jenna were in a corner booth, under one of the faux antique rifles that decorated the log-jammed, rustic interior.

"*What* did he say to you?" Jenna asked from across the booth, sitting next to Tammy.

Both women were as wide-eyed as Donna had been after his confession.

"He said what he's feeling is 'the real thing.'" Donna shook her head. "Luckily, he didn't push the subject on the ride home or when he dropped me off, but I know he's still got this mistaken impression about…well, whatever he thinks he's feeling for me."

Tammy and Jenna traded glances. Then her sister said, "It's love, you doofus!"

Donna sank down a bit in her seat. "That's not what he meant." He couldn't have.

Tammy disagreed. "And here I thought *I* was the innocent one in this group. You act like you've never had a man tell you he loves you, Donna."

This was the very definition of mortifying. But Donna was beyond lying to them. She genuinely needed some advice.

"I…haven't had anyone say that to me before."

Both women gaped.

"Oh, don't give me those looks like, 'Isn't that so sad? Poor Donna.' Because I was never looking for love. I'm still not."

Jenna stirred the straw in her cherry cola as if she was attempting to bring the conversation down a notch. "Love sure came to you, though."

Donna stared at her untouched salad. Time to get real.

"So here I am," she said softly. "Someone who has no idea what to do with deep feelings. And there he is—a well-known good-time guy who's the same way."

"Wait." Tammy had just piled lettuce onto her Buffalo Bill burger. "How do you know that Caleb has no idea what love is like?"

Donna glanced around the near-empty diner. It was off-hours, so only a few customers ate in their booths on the other side of the room. Caleb's name had seemed to echo, though.

But maybe she was just hearing his name all around her, bouncing off every wall…including the ones around her heart.

Jenna spoke. "You're making excuses, saying he doesn't know what love is when you don't know if that's true or not."

Tammy added, "He loves his family enough to take care of them. And Caleb loved Tex."

"Not the same kind of love," Donna said, finally spearing some of her salad.

Jenna rolled her eyes. "Excuses, excuses."

"That may be so, but does that mean there's any kind of future for me with Caleb Granger?"

She shoved a bite of salad into her mouth, not tasting any of it, because there was one word she'd said that stood out from the others.

The future. *Her in a field, on a blanket, her hand on her rounding belly...*

She had a hard time swallowing, and one of those furious blushes consumed her, but this one was exponentially worse than any she'd dealt with before as she remembered the mattress dream.

Had fate already dictated her future? Because that had definitely been the case with both Tammy and Jenna.

But there was absolutely no way she'd ever be pregnant. They'd used a condom, and Donna was not going to sleep with Caleb again.

Donna caught Jenna and Tammy looking at each other once more.

Then Jenna said, "Did you just freak out a little on us, sis? You mentioned one little word—*future*—and you started blushing and nearly choking on your food as if you've *seen* your future. Is that because you two spent the night on the feather bed?"

Tammy set down her burger.

Wonderful. Now she had this to deal with, too. "Who told you two about me and Caleb and the dream cabin?"

Jenna spoke up. "First of all, you two left Lone Star Lucy's together, then J.D. went into work earlier than usual and he saw Caleb's truck at the dream cabin. I just want to hear it from you."

"Okay. We did make a stop there."

Tammy asked, "And what exactly happened?"

Jenna poked her with an elbow. "Nosy pants. Only sisters should dig that far into someone's business." She turned to Donna. "And what exactly happened?"

Really. These two should've taken their act on the road. "You guys have fiancés. Surely I don't need to go into the details."

Donna thought that the women might've done a secretive low-five beneath the table.

"Why're you two so ecstatic about it?" Donna asked. The memory of that mattress dream was pulling at her, now that they were talking about it. She'd tried to dismiss it yesterday, but here it was again.

"Because you can be happy," Jenna said. "Remember that list I made naming off the qualities that my perfect man should have?"

"Who can forget?"

"Well," Jenna said, looking rather satisfied, "it turns out that all my plans on that list were for nothing. I didn't see J.D. coming, but here we are."

She flashed her diamond engagement ring, and Donna couldn't help smiling.

Still, she wasn't going down easy. "You always were more adaptable than I was."

"Not by much."

Tammy broke in. "Can we please get back to what happened in that cabin? And I'm not talking about the nitty-gritty. You slept on that mattress, so did you have any dreams like we did?"

"I don't remember."

Jenna wadded up her napkin and threw it at Donna. It hit her in the forehead.

"Hey," Donna said. "I have no dreams to report."

As Jenna and Tammy frowned in disappointment, Donna told herself not to feel bad about lying to them. Why even relate something that was never ever going to come true, anyway?

Donna Byrd with a baby.

Inconceivable. Even if she sometimes felt that empty space inside of her pulsing.

They finished up their meal, then drove back to the ranch. Jenna and Tammy sang to the radio like teeny-boppers, making Donna smile. Someday, when she was back in the city, she would invite these two to stay with her, and they'd have a real girls' night out on the town.

Tammy pulled her pickup in front of the main house, where there were two familiar cars parked in front of the porch.

One was a classic Trans Am, the other a white, stylish Cadillac.

It seemed as if the air went still. Jenna even rested her hand on Donna's shoulder in solidarity.

"Do you think," she said, "Uncle William and Dad are even in the same room right now?"

"Why wouldn't they be?" Donna asked. "They've been working on getting along."

"But the news about James," Tammy said. "It made things kind of tense again, set them back a little."

Donna barely heard the girls, because Caleb's voice was dominating her head. *If you have the chance to make things right, Donna, take it. You never know when it'll be too late...*

As usual, he was right, because she couldn't stand

the notion of avoiding her dad, or even sitting across the dinner table from him with neither one of them recognizing the elephant in the room.

All the issues between them.

Donna was the first out of Tammy's pickup, and she went straight for the door.

She found Uncle William, Aidan and Nathan sitting in the living room drinking bourbon, relaxing and chatting.

After saying hi, then giving her gray-haired uncle a welcoming hug, she asked, "Do you know where my dad is?"

William took a drink of his liquor, not revealing a thing about the status between the twin brothers. But Nathan gestured toward the exit with his cut crystal glass.

"Try the kitchen. He went straight for it, saying he wanted to fill his stomach before he joined us for a drink."

Or maybe, Donna thought, Dad still wasn't on perfect terms with his brother, thanks to the James discovery.

She passed Jenna and Tammy in the entryway and gently took her sister's arm, pulling her down the hallway.

"What's going on?" Jenna asked.

"You'll probably want to see Dad before I say my piece."

When Jenna began to utter something, Donna interrupted. "I'm getting this over with once and for all, Jenna. I can't stand another second of it."

At the kitchen door, she didn't hesitate—she pushed it open to find their father at the nook table, huddled over a plate with a ham sandwich that'd barely been eaten.

His eyes, which had always been such a bright blue,

were faded to the color of jeans that'd been carelessly left in the sun, but he was as handsome and imposing as ever with that graying brown hair and exercise-honed physique.

Jenna went over to say her hellos, then with a good-luck glance at Donna, who was lingering by the window, she sent one more smile over to Dad and left the room.

The air just hung there, heavy and loaded, until Dad gestured to the seat across from him.

"I expect you're here to give me an earful like Jenna once did."

She was trying so hard not to give in to all the anger, and she straightened her spine, going to the chair and sitting.

*If you have the chance to make things right*...said Caleb's voice again.

Donna pushed that anger aside, finally facing the father who'd so bitterly disappointed her.

## *Chapter Nine*

Sam spoke first as he grabbed the napkin from his lap and put it on the table. "I readied myself for this. I've been getting it from all sides lately."

Donna's temper flared. She didn't want to hear excuses.

But then she thought of Caleb again.

"I'm not here to point out blame," she said. "And I'm not going to ask you to rehash everything you told Jenna about what happened with Savannah all those years ago. She's told me everything."

"I figured she would." A slight smile got to him, even though his gaze was still faded. "You two have become closer."

"Yes. That's one positive angle in of all this." And there'd been Tex. There was another, too, but she wasn't going to tell him about Caleb. He hadn't earned it.

Then again, why would she announce anything about Caleb to her father when there was nothing major there?

He started up again. "I should have paid more attention to you and Jenna when you were growing up. It's only now, after I've spent time with William again, that I see what we all lost over the years with family. Brothers and sisters should never have a distance between them. Tex came to that realization, too."

"Jenna and I weren't estranged, like you and Uncle William. We were just…"

"Seemingly indifferent."

"No, that was me. Jenna knew how to express emotions as well as she could in our house."

Sam shook his head. "That was definitely my fault. I had my head in my business so far that I didn't see how your mom's sickness affected you both. I didn't see how our divorce made you, especially, pull into a shelter that you rarely came out of, except to design your little girl magazines and decorate those shoe boxes like they were tiny rooms in a house."

"Dioramas." Her chest tightened. "That's what they were called."

When he smiled, it was almost as if Donna was back in the days when his approval meant everything to her. That hurt more than anything.

"Yes," he said. "You'd buy scrap material from the store and use it for wallpaper and bedspreads. And you used to make paper people out of tissue. They lived in those rooms."

"I remember." She'd always been goal-oriented, even when she was in grade school.

"And look at you now—still decorating those rooms,

but on a much larger scale. Still putting together magazines, too."

She used to hope for moments like this, but they had come so much harder from him. She would carry those dioramas and magazines into his home office after her parents had divorced and she and Jenna would visit him on the weekends. He would reluctantly pull himself away from whatever report he was going over, then look at her efforts, making suggestions here and there that she would implement immediately.

Approval had been her idea of love. Of course, Mom had given affection more freely—she'd fawned over each of her daughter's creations. Donna had valued that, too, although she'd been in such a shell from the divorce that she hadn't known how to handle the hugs Mom tried to give her, the kisses.

And when Mom had gone, Donna had regretted the way she'd treated her so much that she'd fallen even further into that shell.

Donna risked a glance at her father. He was watching her with such melancholy that she almost forgot all her frustration with him then and there.

"You really blew it, didn't you?" she asked softly. "And I'm not just talking about with Savannah, William and Grandpa."

"You're talking about your mom." There were faint red circles under his eyes that Donna had just noticed. "As I told Jenna, when I met your mom, it was on the tail of my relationship with Savannah. I was a mess, but your mom was drawn to a brokenhearted bad boy. She was never able to change me from that to a good husband, though."

"She thought she could? That's why she married you so quickly after your breakup with Savannah?"

"Yes. But doesn't every woman in love think that they're the only one who can fix what's broken in a man?"

Donna almost told him no—she was a perfect example of the opposite. But there were definitely men out there who thought they knew how to mend a woman they'd fallen for.

Caleb, for one.

Some of the heaviness rolled off her, just at the thought of him.

She saw her dad measuring her with his gaze, but she didn't want him to see that what he'd said had struck her in a meaningful way.

"So here we are," she said, sitting back in her chair.

He nodded. "Here we are."

Was this enough to repair their relationship? She didn't think so. There were still so many questions to be asked and solved.

"What're you going to do if Savannah ever calls back and says she and James are paying us a visit?" she asked.

Sam ran a hand through his hair. "I know that after Tammy found the grocery receipt with the pregnancy test on it in Savannah's cabin, I told your sister I hoped that Savannah didn't get pregnant. I wouldn't be able to look at the child if he was William's—a child would be a reminder of how Savannah and my brother had been together and how he'd felt about her."

"And you told Jenna that you were such a crummy parent to us that you didn't want to be one a third time to a possible child." Donna's tone darkened. "You know that you don't have a choice now, and I swear to God, if you shirk this duty as James' uncle or his father, I'm never going to forgive you."

It was as if she'd reached inside of him to pull his heart out.

The daughter he loved, leaving him just as he and William had left Tex.

She hadn't realized the parallel until now, and she wanted to take it back.

But he saved her from doing that. "I've had time to think," he said. "William gave me a lot of perspective on this last trip. And when you kids called us with the definite news about James…"

*Please don't disappoint me,* she thought. *I don't know what I'll do if you put this final nail in me.*

He sighed. "I can't get James off my mind. But no matter how much I think about him, it's impossible to predict how I'd feel about knowing who he belongs to, one way or another."

"It sounds to me like James is the type of person who feels as if he doesn't belong to any kind of father. I suspect he's the one holding up Savannah's phone call." Donna frowned. "But you're going to welcome him into the family, no matter what. Just tell me that much, Dad."

Again, he got that decimated look that said he'd never wanted to hurt Donna or Jenna. That he was full of remorse, and he just wasn't sure how to go about reaching a reckoning with himself.

At that moment, Donna realized that her father needed her, just as much as Caleb's needed him. Maybe Mr. Granger wasn't capable of admitting it, but Sam was doing so as he reached across the table to her.

She didn't have it in her to turn him away, ice queen or not.

Touching her fingers to the top of his hand, she said, "How will it feel to see Savannah again?"

A haunted cloud passed over his gaze before he averted it toward the window, and Donna's heart softened even more.

Did he still love Savannah?

She grasped his hand all the way, and as he turned his gaze to her, she saw that it'd gotten a little brighter at her willingness to make things right between them.

The weekend arrived, bringing with it a partial day off for Caleb.

It'd been a long couple of days, because, although Donna and he had texted a few times about trivial things—how the visit with her dad was going, how her plans for the staff party today were shaping up—he hadn't seen her around.

He'd vowed to back off, because at this point, if this relationship was meant to be, she would come to him.

Right?

But she'd better do it soon, he thought, as he drove his truck toward Dad and Aunt Rosemary's house, because the first thing this morning, Hugh had pulled him aside and told him that he was going on an extended trip than included an out-of-state agricultural business conference and then several visits to state-of-the-art ranches.

And Caleb would be leaving tomorrow morning.

"I got you registered at the last minute, and I just received confirmation," Hugh had said. "Sorry for the late notice."

"Isn't this something you'd rather go to?" Caleb had asked, thinking of how long this would keep him away from Donna.

"Don't worry—your girl will still be here when you get back. And absence might make her heart grow fonder. Besides, Tex always meant for you to take my place, and I'd like you to be up on all the latest business when that happens."

A sense of pride had bolstered Caleb, but then again, what *about* Donna? He would be gone for a few weeks altogether with both the conference and the ranch trips and he wondered what she'd say when he told her about that.

Would she be relieved that she'd finally gotten rid of him?

He was still mulling it over late that afternoon when he arrived at Dad and Aunt Rosemary's, where they were already waiting for him to pick them up for the Flying B's party.

Or, at least, Rosemary was waiting.

She was outside the open garage, where his father's old green Dodge Aspen was stored. Her thin arms were crossed over her chest, her long polka-dot skirt blowing in the slight wind.

Caleb could already see it was another not-so-good day.

He parked his truck to the side of the driveway, got out, then greeted Rosemary.

She canted her head toward the car in the garage, and he could make out in the shadows that Dad was sitting in the driver's seat.

"He's all ready to go," she said.

"Does he think he's driving?"

"That's what he's demanding."

She didn't have to add that she'd had no idea what

she'd been in for when she'd volunteered to look after Dad. But what caretaker did know?

*It's not his fault,* Caleb kept thinking. *He's only still trying his best to feel as if he's in control.*

A ball of wariness shaped itself into Caleb's gut. What would it be like to lose yourself like this?

All he knew was that life was too short, and maybe that's why he'd gone after Donna full force after he'd decided so strongly that she was the one for him. Maybe Dad and Tex had shown him that you didn't have all the time in the world.

Caleb girded himself and sauntered over to the driver's side of the car.

"Hi, Dad."

When he glanced at Caleb, it was obvious that he'd shined himself up for the party. His gray hair was combed back, nice and neat, and he was wearing a spiffy Western shirt and black jeans and boots, no stains in sight.

The excited gleam in his eyes surprised Caleb. He'd expected meanness, not this.

"I'm ready," Dad said. "Got the keys with you?"

Caleb glanced at Rosemary, who'd come to his side. She wore a smile now, as if she was just as happy to see Dad in this sudden good mood as Caleb was.

Had Caleb put that smile on his face?

His heart expanded, then went back to its normal size when he started thinking about how to sustain Dad's levity.

"Here's the thing, Dad," Caleb said. "The Aspen needs some repairs. How about we take my truck today?"

"I can repair this baby. What needs to be done?" Dad

frowned, as if racking his brain for memories of what might've been ailing his treasured car.

Caleb felt terrible for lying to him, but as it was, Rosemary had to hide the keys so Dad wouldn't be a menace on the road.

"I'll tell you what needs to be done after we get back," Caleb said, opening the door, treading lightly. "See, there's a barbecue where we're expected. Ribs galore."

"Oh." That got Dad out of the car. "Kathy doesn't like to be late to functions. Better get a move on."

Kathy had been Caleb's mom, and the reminder that Dad wasn't quite in the present again was just another smackdown.

One good moment, one step back. But Caleb wouldn't have traded today's good moment for anything.

After they were all in Caleb's truck, Dad in the middle and Rosemary by the door, the ride to the Flying B was pleasant enough. Dad talked about the "functions" he and Mom had gone to back in the day, and Caleb only prayed that he wouldn't ask just where Kathy was right now.

Thank God he didn't. And after they arrived in front of the main house of the ranch, with a banner saying, "Welcome to the Flying B and B!" stretched over the porch, Dad wandered straight over to the line of picnic benches that moaned under a buffet of Texas food. Staff members—including the ranch hands who'd taken a meal break from running the cattle operation to the housemaids to the cowboys and cowgirls who'd be facilitating the outdoor activities for the B and B—mingled. The sweet-smoky scent of barbecue tickled the air, along with the sound check that a local band was doing on a stage that had been set up.

Aunt Rosemary touched Caleb's arm, smiling at him, then she followed Dad to the refreshments.

It was nice to see her having a good day, too.

As he was watching after them, he felt someone come to his side. The goose bumps up and down his arm told him who it was.

"Donna," he said.

Just one look at her made it an even better day.

She was wearing a dark pink sundress that looked like it'd been culled out of a '50s catalog. But the old-fashioned style suited her, hugging her curves, making her upswept hairdo seem chic and down-home at the same time.

His blood pumped, as if filling him with all that color she brought with her, just by being in the same place he was.

"Is that your father and aunt?" she asked.

"It is."

"I'm glad he was well enough to be here."

"I'll introduce you as soon as he's done loading up on the goodies."

He looked into those blue-sky eyes of hers. "You've been busier than usual this week."

"I was getting this party in shape. And if you're asking me for an update on Savannah and James, I don't have one. I've been debating whether to call her again or just take this as a sign that she's not ever going to contact us and neither is James." She threw her hands up in the air. "What can I do but enjoy today, right? What do you guys say in Texas? Yippee ki-yay?"

"We don't really say that."

"But it sounds so fun."

Donna was actually...chipper. "Have you had one of those Ruby cocktails or something?"

She laughed, and as it faded, he could tell she had something else on her mind.

"I wanted to thank you for something, Caleb."

He stopped joking around.

She said, "I mentioned in a text that I had a talk with my dad. I didn't tell you that we're on firmer ground now. Everything's not perfect, but we're communicating. It's a start."

"I'm glad to hear that."

"It's a credit to you that it happened. I kept hearing your words of wisdom, and they calmed me down when I needed it the most."

Had she just admitted that he...mattered to her? Even in some small way?

Across the yard, he saw Dad and Aunt Rosemary taking a seat in padded lounge chairs. His dad's plate was piled with a mound of meat with a cupcake on top while Rosemary's looked like a patch of garden.

"Come on," Caleb said. "I want you to meet my family."

Donna's smile was tentative, as if she wondered what exactly that meant, meeting the family. To him, it meant he was introducing them to his future. But Donna didn't have to know that right now.

He brought her over, then ushered her into an available chair next to Dad while still standing himself.

"This is Donna," he said. "She put this shindig together and is one of the Byrds who's running the B and B."

While Rosemary flashed a brilliant smile at Donna, then a more subtle, curious one at Caleb, Dad finished chewing on some ribs, still as happy as could be.

"Hi, Donna."

It didn't matter that Dad had a searching look in his eyes that told Caleb he had no idea who the Byrds were and probably never would, even if Donna was introduced fifty times over. All that mattered was that Donna and he began chatting about food, laughing about the Red Velvet cupcake that he'd balanced on top of his ribs.

All the while, Rosemary kept giving Caleb the eye, and he shrugged.

*Tell you later.*

When it became hot enough for the misters to spray the crowd in front of the music stage, where the band was ready to strike it up, Donna had to excuse herself.

"Here's where the logistics come in," she said as Caleb escorted her away from his family. "Gotta keep this shindig running smoothly."

"See you in a while," he said. "And I mean that in a few ways."

"Like…how?"

He would just mention the business conference. If she cared, she cared. If she didn't…

He put it out there. "In the morning, I'm off to an ag business conference for about a week, then an extended tour of some high-tech ranches across the state, just to keep up with the times. I'll be gone for a few weeks."

She blinked. "A few weeks."

Bull's-eye. She didn't even have time to cover up the dismay he'd seen in her gaze and heard in her voice.

"It's not forever, Donna."

"No, but…" This time, she did recover. "I'm sure the staff will miss you."

"I'm sure they will."

He tried not to smile as she walked away, toward the stage.

He spent the rest of the afternoon making sure Rosemary and Dad were comfortable, but he knew the good times wouldn't last forever. It was clear Dad was tired a couple hours in, and Caleb asked Rosemary if they were set to go back home.

"Definitely," she said. "I think he'll even fall asleep in the truck."

He certainly did, snoring, overriding the radio that Caleb had turned on before giving up and snapping it off, much to Rosemary's amusement.

When they got to their place, Caleb took care of getting Dad to bed.

That was when they hit the big glitch in their day.

As Caleb was easing Dad down onto his mattress, the old man awoke with a start, then reared away from Caleb and onto the bed, obviously not recognizing him.

"It's all right," Caleb said, holding up his hands. "It's Caleb. Your son."

Before Dad fell back asleep, he gave Caleb a nasty look, no doubt because he was thinking those terrible thoughts about him.

But he did float off right away, and Caleb met Aunt Rosemary in the kitchen, where she offered him some lemonade.

"No, thanks." He wasn't going to mention what'd just happened with Dad. It was par for the course. "I'll be getting back to the ranch."

"Back to Donna," Rosemary said, a glint in her eyes.

Caleb kissed her on the cheek and prepared to bail. "That's a conversation for another time."

"I look forward to it, because from the way you were

looking at her, I get the feeling she's more than one of your…"

"Distractions?"

"That's a fine way of putting it. And she looked at you the same way you did her."

The ground seemed to shake under his feet. He didn't even have the grace to play it cool. "She did?"

"Oh." Aunt Rosemary came to pat him on the face. "It's finally happened, hasn't it?"

Caleb smiled as she hugged him.

Falling head over heels had finally happened to him, but how long would it take for it to happen to Donna?

As dusk enveloped the ranch and the music from the country band played on, Donna sat away from most of the crowd, on the main house's porch, surveying the party from a chair.

Everyone seemed to be having the time of their lives, swinging to a song by a singer she'd recently come to know as Toby Keith. Tammy and Mike were out there, and so were Jenna and J.D. Dad and Uncle William were even sharing a beer by the barn. They were obviously having another of their heart-to-hearts.

It stank not having someone she could dance with or talk to. She already missed not having Caleb around.

But, just as if she'd conjured him out of thin air, he ambled from around the corner of the house, probably from where he'd parked his truck.

She couldn't stop the smile that overwhelmed her, but she sure did calm it down as she stood from the chair. "Your dad and aunt are back home, safe and sound?"

"Dad's in a food coma, but he left happy, that's for sure."

"It was good to meet him and Rosemary today."

"They thought the same with you."

The Toby Keith song ended, easing into something like a Texas waltz.

She licked her lips, her pulse kicking her. Why did she all of a sudden feel shy around Caleb? Because she'd never been introduced to a man's family as she'd been introduced to his? Because, from the time she'd met him until now, something had definitely changed and she couldn't deny it any longer?

Today, she'd seen a quality in him that she'd never gotten to witness before—the way he looked at his dad, protective and caring and concerned. The way he treated his aunt Rosemary as if she were a lady and he appreciated every moment she took in taking care of the family.

Caleb was the real deal, she thought. And he was standing right here next to her, reaching out a hand.

"At Lone Star Lucy's," he said, "you never did get on the dance floor."

Was he asking her to do so now? In front of everyone?

But why was that such a big thing when the whole ranch was gossiping about them, anyway? And how was a dance somehow more intimate than what they'd done on that feather bed?

A flash of her mattress dream rattled her again, but she ignored it, just as she did his outstretched hand.

"This isn't my kind of music," she said. Lame.

"It's easy to dance to." Without waiting, he took her hand in his, resting the other one on her hip. "You just sway, Donna. That's all."

In spite of herself, she'd come to place her fingers on his arm. She felt skin and muscle underneath his shirt. Felt *him*.

Her heartbeat took off like a fearful creature, seeking cover.

"I've never been any good at this," she said.

"Dancing?" His voice was low, like a caress skimming her.

"No. I've never been good at relating."

"You mean relationships."

"Both."

He laughed. "You've already warned me."

She was going to lay it all out in a last-ditch attempt to get him to understand that she wasn't cut out for him, for this, no matter what she was starting to feel.

"First," she said, "there was my parents' divorce. That's never a good thing for a kid to go through. Then, my mom's death. I learned early that I was the only one who'd always be there for myself."

Caleb pulled her a little closer as they swayed, and she absently adjusted her hand higher up his arm.

"I always had this vague feeling that Dad never talked about Grandpa because something had gone terribly wrong," she said. "Dad had this black-sheep vibe, and it's something I sort of adopted. That's why I've never had any serious relationships, Caleb."

"There's a time for everything," he said.

"How can you be so cavalier about what I just told you? Haven't I given you enough to frighten you off?"

He smiled down at her. "You've given me enough to make life interesting."

"I don't think you need a more interesting life."

"Not in the way you're talking about." He squeezed her tighter. "I want to live, Donna. Tex wanted that for me, too, and every time I see my dad, I get that much more determined to start the rest of my life as soon as I can."

"You should do it with a nice girl."

"You are a nice one. You just don't know it yet."

He'd told her that they never really knew who their parents were—but did that go for them, too? Because she really did feel different around Caleb.

She was trying so hard to love the person her dad had become these days, so why was it impossible that Caleb could love the woman *he'd* come to know in her, even if she didn't think of herself that way?

Without analyzing a second more, she threw caution to the wind, stood on her tiptoes and pressed her lips to Caleb's.

They stopped dancing, but the waltz in her head kept on playing, swirling, sweeping down through her. She pulled him close, not wanting him to go to that conference and ranch tour that would take him away for a few weeks.

Not wanting him to go anywhere.

But then, as she pulled away and looked into his gaze, she saw the hope she'd just planted in him, and it killed her.

She'd been impulsive, and even though she shouldn't be giving anyone hope, she wanted some of it for herself so badly.

But he seemed to read on her face that she was caught between emotions that she couldn't quite grasp, and he let her go.

He tipped his hat to her, just like the gentlemen he'd never seemed to be, but was.

"It'll only be a few weeks, Donna," he said. "I'll be back before you know it, so no shenanigans, you hear?"

Then he walked off the porch, leaving her wanting even more from him.

And she suspected that's what he'd been hoping for all along.

## *Chapter Ten*

Three weeks seemed like forever to Donna. They felt more like three aeons, even though she'd been tied up with visits from travel agents and magazine writers who would hopefully be recommending the Flying B and B after it opened in a little over a few weeks.

They already had the first month booked, thanks to her college friend Theo's published magazine article, but it was still a stressful time.

At first, that was why Donna thought she missed her period. Because of the stress.

And it wasn't until she started to think about the pregnancy dream she'd had in the cabin again that she wondered, even doubtfully, if there might be something else going on.

So she turned to the only person she felt comfortable in telling her worries to these days, asking Jenna to meet her in her room.

When her sister knocked on the door, Donna opened it right away and ushered her inside. Jenna's blond hair was in a braid down her back, and in her dark blue Western shirt and jeans, she looked as if she had always belonged here, on a ranch. But Donna, herself, must've appeared as nervous as a stray cat who'd blundered into a dog pound, because Jenna immediately asked, "My, God, what's wrong? Did Savannah call?"

"No."

Savannah had actually left one message for them, saying that she was still talking things out with James and she would be in touch again either way. Donna had almost called the woman back, but she didn't want to harass her.

*Give them time,* she kept thinking. Even so, the Byrds were beginning to accept that they might have run into a dead end.

And maybe it was for the best if Savannah and James wanted nothing to do with them.

"What's wrong then?" Jenna asked.

Donna went to her dresser, pulling out a bag with the name of the town's drugstore spelled out over the white paper.

Then she took out what was inside the bag.

When Jenna saw the boxed pregnancy test, she was speechless.

"I never miss my period," Donna said. "Not until lately."

Her fearful tone apparently put Jenna into action, and she came over to touch Donna's arm.

"You're scared, aren't you."

"A little bit." But there was more to it than that. A

wad of nerves actually was spinning in the center of her, but there was excitement, too.

Donna hadn't expected that.

*A baby,* she kept thinking. *And me, as a mother.*

But even with her doubts, something fluttery in her kept awakening.

*Could* she be a mom?

Donna knit her brows. The empty place inside of her that she'd felt before hadn't existed for the past couple of days. Warmth had taken its place, like a soft bundle nestling at the core of her.

Unexpected, all right. Yet it felt like the most natural thing in the world right now.

"I never knew I wanted a baby," she said to Jenna.

Her sister hugged her until reality invaded Donna again.

"I don't know if the timing is where I would've wanted it to be," she said. "My investments are shrinking by the day, and that's not an optimal situation for raising a child. And then there's the matter of who the father is…"

"Caleb."

Just hearing his name sent a pang through her. She'd missed his laugh, his smile, his easy way of making her feel as if she could slow down for once and see a different part of herself with him.

But, as Donna glanced at the test in her hand, more doubt shaded her. Just because she and Caleb might be having a child, that didn't make everything okay. It didn't make all their issues magically dissolve.

"I've had good times with him," Donna said. "But this is a curveball. We used a condom, Jen. So how did this happen?"

"It must've leaked."

"I couldn't tell."

Jenna held Donna's hand. "Don't think I'm selfish, but I would love to be an aunt. And you'd be a great mother, even if you might not think so."

"Would I?"

Jenna pulled back and peered into Donna's eyes. "You think you're such a tough cookie, but you've got a core of butter."

"I do not." Donna laughed a bit, but she was on the edge of tears, too.

She was about to get news that might change her life...and Caleb's.

*A baby,* she kept thinking, but this time, she couldn't stop a genuine smile. True, it wavered, but there it was. And, for the first time ever in her rush-around life, she took the time to imagine what it could feel like to hold someone who thought she was the entire world, someone she would give her life for.

Powdery smells, a nursery, a quiet night in a rocker, singing lullabies to her son or daughter...

*Yes,* Donna thought. This was what she had been missing. Someone to share every day with.

Then a jarring thought intruded. *But I got pregnant during a one-night stand. Does that mean I'll have to live the rest of my life with Caleb, even if I know a relationship won't work in the long run?*

It was a terrible thought. But it was also a practical one. Yet what was she going to do—run away and never tell Caleb about their child?

The warmth around her heart seemed to burn her, as if trying to tell her something she just wasn't understanding.

Jenna obviously sensed Donna's conflict. "You're still scared."

Her sister was the only one who would ever fully get what Donna was about to say.

"You remember how it felt when Mom and Dad divorced?"

"Like the world was ending."

"Jenna, what if I'm about to set this child up for the same devastation we had to go through?"

Jenna frowned. "Are you already planning to get a divorce from Caleb or something?"

What *was* she saying?

She gripped the pregnancy test in one hand. "I'm only being careful. Trying to think things through, here. You, more than anyone, know how Dad rushed into marriage with Mom. This thing I have with Caleb… It's not even as serious as Dad and Mom supposedly got with one another before they said 'I do.'"

Donna realized she was almost crushing the box. Still, more irrational thoughts swamped her.

*If I am pregnant, should I tell Caleb? Or should I think of the child so he or she can be saved from what's sure to be a dysfunctional relationship for his or her parents?*

A relationship that would mimic the thwarted marriage that had thrown Donna and Jenna into a tailspin for years…

Then another unreasonable notion barged into Donna's head. *Wasn't that what Savannah did with James? She ran away and kept the baby a secret?*

The comparison definitely didn't cheer Donna up. The only thing that was going to either improve the situation or not was taking that test.

She pointed toward the bathroom. "If I go in there, will you stick around until I come out?"

"You bet I will."

Jenna squeezed her hand, and Donna headed for privacy, closing the door.

As she removed the stick from the packaging, it seemed as if time had warped into a speed that was both slow *and* fast, clouding her head. Somehow she managed to take that test.

Then all she could do was wait, and she did so by opening the bathroom door and sitting on the bed with Jenna. The digital alarm clock on the dresser flashed the seconds.

"Thank you for being here, Jen," she said. In the past, it would've been a hard thing for Donna to say. Not anymore.

Jenna smiled, her eyes shiny as she put her arm around Donna. "Of course I'm here. And whatever the outcome, I won't tell anyone."

"Thanks for that, too."

The few minutes that were required for the test had passed, but Donna wasn't moving.

"Are you ready to look?" Jenna asked.

*Was* she ready?

The image of a blue-eyed, dimpled child nuzzled up to Donna again, the warmth in her chest nearly overtaking her now.

She really did want to be ready, more than she had ever thought possible.

But would Caleb turn tail and flee if her test was positive? Maybe the impulsive part of him would consume him, just like the ladies' man he'd been rumored to be, and she could go her own way…with their child.

Donna went into the bathroom, where she'd set the stick in the sink. Jenna was right behind her.

Before Donna peered at it, she did something she hadn't done in a long, long time.

*If it's a yes, God, please have me be the best mom ever.*

She took a huge breath as she checked the marker.

When she saw the smiley face on it, she turned around, heading right into Jenna's waiting arms. As she cried into her sister's hair, she barely got out the words.

"It's a yes," she said.

Jenna started crying, too, yet Donna realized that, like her own sobbing, these were tears of surprising happiness.

*I'm going to have a child,* she thought once more. But, then again, so was Caleb.

A day later, when Caleb returned to the Flying B, he wasted no time in going to the main house, where dusk hovered over the roof like a display of orange, pink and blue feathers.

He'd been aching for Donna for three damned weeks, during every workshop at that conference and during every visit he had paid during the tour of the ranches that were ahead of the mainstream agricultural curve.

It'd been three weeks of torture, but he'd refrained from calling or even texting her.

*Give her room,* he kept thinking. This separation would show him what their future really was.

Half nervous and half elated, he pulled his truck to a skid near the back patio, then got out, straightening his hat and walking right up to the kitchen door, where he knew Barbara would be cleaning up from her dinner prep.

After entering the house, Caleb was caught off guard by the sight of Tammy, who occasionally liked to use the top-of-the-line kitchen to bake goodies for the ranch staff, just as she was doing now with batches of fudge brownies that rested on wire racks and lent the room a sweet aroma.

She wiped at her cheek, leaving a flour mark that matched the ones on her red frilled apron. "You're home!"

Then she came over to give him a friendly punch on the arm, just before cleaning her hands on the apron. Her cute and perky smile remained, though.

"I can get Donna for you," she said.

"That'd be great, Tammy."

She started out of the kitchen, but then hesitated. "You know she's going to act as if she didn't miss you for a second, but I know better. She's been wandering around looking like she lost her dog. Or…you. Or…" She tucked a long dark lock behind her ear and smiled. "Just let me go get her."

"Thanks." Caleb stayed by the door, taking off his hat and smoothing back his hair.

The last time he'd felt like this, he'd been taking Kelly Tartleton to the prom and standing in her family room with her corsage. Luckily, by the end of the night, the nerves had worn off, just as quickly as Kelly's fancy dress.

But memories of prom smoked away when Donna arrived, garbed in one of her sundresses. She was like a breath of the fresh Flying B air he'd missed—fragrant and bringing with it just a touch of humidity.

And she was alone, bless Tammy.

The girl had been right about Donna's standoff-ishness, though—she was waiting on one side of the kitchen, him on the other, although Caleb was pretty sure that she was telling herself not to look too excited.

Unfortunately for her, her bright gaze betrayed her. Those blue eyes were shining, even if she was resting her hand on her stomach in a posture he'd never caught her in before.

Was it because her stomach was somersaulting, just as his was?

A beat passed, and he wondered if she was about to throw herself into his arms.

But then she smiled, almost shyly, and it captured his heart. Still, there was something else about her...

"You're back," she said.

"It had to happen sometime."

"How was the trip?"

"Long." He took a step toward her. "Too long."

It was as if she was searching for something to say that would keep him on the other side of the room. Would he have to start all over again with winning her over?

Hell, he was sucker enough to do it.

"Your family?" she asked. "Have you seen them yet?"

He wanted to say he had come here first because he couldn't stay away another minute. But, dammit, he'd realized long ago that Donna needed slow.

She couldn't be pushed.

"I'll be going to Dad and Aunt Rosemary's tonight," he said. "She's expecting me, at least."

"You could've gone to see them first."

It was as if she had thrown a wall between them,

and he exhaled a long breath. Then he said, "Maybe I should have."

He hadn't meant that. It'd just been frustration speaking.

Donna had her hand over her stomach again, as if shielding herself. She sat in a chair at a small table.

Cursing under his breath, Caleb said, "As I mentioned, I wanted to be here first."

She gestured to a chair, and when he sat, her gaze was serious in a way he'd never seen before—puzzled, as if she was putting together a thousand pieces in her mind and he wasn't fitting anywhere.

"If you could talk to your dad and he understood every word," she asked, "what would you say to him, Caleb?"

Odd question. Then again, this was Donna. She would be coming around to some kind of point, probably about her own dad. Maybe they'd had it out today and that was the reason for her distance.

"I don't know what I'd say to him." Caleb laid a hand on top of his hat as it rested in his lap. "I suppose I'd ask Dad if he ever changed his mind about me from when I was a kid until now. And, if I got brave, I might ask if he meant to be so remote with me when I was growing up. If he disliked me for some reason besides the trouble I gave him."

"What do you think of the way your dad raised you?"

What was this? Twenty disquieting questions?

"I'd do things a little different than him," he said. "I'd take the time to see what it was my son or daughter was doing every day and involve myself, even just a little. But I wouldn't interfere or hover. Not unless they wanted me to. And I wouldn't think I was acting strong by being emotionally distant."

She sat back in her chair, that weird look still on her face. She was picking at the edge of the table, too, as if she were fretful.

"With my dad," he said, "strength was always a big thing, and I think he'd be decimated to realize that he's lost it now with his dementia. I would be the same, though. It scares me to think that anyone could become a shadow of what they used to be."

It seemed as if she wanted to ask him more questions, but she was holding back.

Yet when she glanced at him again, he saw something else in her eyes—a longing.

Was she dying to touch him as much as he was her?

"Donna," he said, "aren't you the one who kissed me goodbye before I left, or was I imagining that?"

"You weren't."

"Have things changed so much while I've been gone?"

She blanched, then stood very slowly.

"I guess they have," he said.

"Caleb, I just need to figure a few things out…."

*Patience,* he thought. He'd told himself he could wait. But for how long?

He stood, too, putting on his hat. "I'm not a man who rushes, Donna. You know that. But I don't linger around forever, either."

Her gaze went shadowy, as if he'd played right into every one of her Donna-Byrd neuroses about her parents' divorce and her mother's death and being abandoned.

"Thanks for seeing me first, Caleb," she said, averting her face so he couldn't read her at all.

As she left the kitchen, she sent him one last look over

her shoulder, and it was almost enough to take him to his knees with its yearning.

But then it was gone, just as she was.

Maybe frustration was a ranch hand's best friend, because it sure kept Caleb's mind off Donna the next day as he worked his fingers to the bone in the cattle fields, maintaining those pipes and ditches from sunup to sundown.

He hardly even talked to anyone he was so busy... until he found Hugh sitting on the porch after dinner, just as Caleb was walking toward his cabin in the fallen night.

"You're doing a real fine job," Hugh said from a pine rocker, smoking a pipeful of cherry tobacco under the lantern by the door.

"Are you sure about that?" Caleb said, thinking of Donna, as always.

Hugh laughed. "I'm just telling you that you're gonna be a good foreman. It's always been clear that the fellows like you, they look up to you and they see that you'll work every corner of this ranch without complaint. Plus, you're now the most technology-savvy cowboy we've got, after that conference and ranch tour. I expect you'll be putting the stuff you learned into practice."

J.D. had been right about Hugh's intentions after all. "I expect so."

Puffing away on that pipe, Hugh gestured for Caleb to join him, just as if it were his own cabin he was lollygagging at. Nevertheless, Caleb climbed the steps of his porch, then leaned back against the railing, smelling the tobacco and summer grass around them.

Hugh inspected him with a squinty gaze.

"What?" Caleb asked.

"I told you that Miss Donna Byrd was going to give you headaches." *Now* Hugh was talking about her. "She's skittish, ain't she?"

"There's actually got to be another word for Donna's kind of skittish. She goes beyond it."

Hugh peered into the distance. "I'll tell you what— if I'd been shy and unassuming with my Minnie, we would've never gotten anywhere. She wasn't as stubborn and high-falutin' as Donna, but she gave me a run for my money. I suppose I can't fault you for your persistence."

Minnie had been Hugh's wife for about four decades. She'd passed on five years ago, and Hugh had never looked at another woman since.

Caleb rested his hands on his hips. "I'll bet Minnie wasn't half as ornery as Donna."

"Oh, you'd be wrong about that. Minnie made me jump through hoops like a show horse, and it wasn't until she realized that I was sincere that she gave me what I'd been hoping for. I knew there was no other woman for me. Isn't that how you feel about Donna?"

Caleb grinned. "Yeah, it is."

"Then even if I once had reservations, there's nothing I'd like to see more than you getting your heart's desire, no matter how skittish Donna gets. From what I've seen and heard, you've made more headway with her than I ever expected. Don't waste that kind of progress, Caleb. Do our mankind proud."

"If you came here to cheer me up after a long day, you're doing a good job."

The sound of a vehicle growled in the near distance, and Hugh took the pipe out of his mouth while standing from the rocker. Then he nodded toward the road that passed by the cabins.

There was a ranch-issued Dodge truck coming at them, and when Donna Byrd cut the engine and got out, Caleb could've been knocked over with a twig.

As Hugh passed by, he wagged his pipe at Caleb and loudly whispered, "Speak of the she-devil."

Then he winked and tapped out the tobacco to the ground before deserting the porch.

He tipped his hat to Donna while heading for his cabin, and she watched him go, then nudged at the ground with the toe of her sandal. She looked up at Caleb, contrition in her gaze.

"Looks like I caught you on your way in for the night."

He gestured toward the porch but she shook her head. "I don't have a great reason to stop by. I just…did."

When she tugged at the front of her sundress, as if there was something about it that wasn't fitting—even though it did—he frowned.

"I expect you're going to say what you have to say to me sometime tonight, Donna."

Now she met his gaze straight-on, just as if she was ready to finally come to terms with him.

Last night, when Caleb had stopped by to see Donna, she hadn't quite been prepared for him.

Then again, she was fairly certain she would never be—not with the news she knew she should be telling him, but couldn't. For privacy's sake, she had even gone out of the county to a doctor's appointment, avoiding Tammy's fiancé, Mike. The other doctor had confirmed the pregnancy.

So what excuse did she have now?

Nonetheless, excuses kept coming up: she should really give Caleb some time to get back into his routine before turning his life upside down. Also, Caleb was probably too busy with his dad to give his full attention to her, anyway.

But when she had asked him about being a father last night, she'd done it to test him. And the answers he'd given her were touching.

They were also right.

Tonight, she'd wanted only more reassuring answers from him, because this was the most momentous thing that had ever happened to her, and she'd sat in bed since she'd taken that pregnancy test, cupping her tummy just as she had in her mattress dream, although she wasn't as round as she'd been in that particular image. Not yet.

*Was* Caleb father material?

Or would all his attraction-at-first-sight games end, making him run away now that matters had become very real?

"I just came here to ask you something," she said. "And please don't take this as anything more than a question, Caleb."

"I won't."

Okay. So far, so good.

"If there *were* a future between us—and I'm not saying there is—but if there were…how would it work out?"

Hope lit his gaze, but he didn't revert to the charming smile he'd always used on her. This was a sincere look that gripped her heart and soul.

"There're options," he said, leaning against the porch pole. "It looks like they want to make me foreman of the Flying B."

"So you'd want to stay here."

"Not necessarily. I'm not just a country boy, Donna. If you wanted me in the city, I'd damned well go to the city and find something to do there. God knows what, but I've always been pretty fast at learning."

She could feel the tears starting to gather in her eyes. This man *had* to be too good to be true. Surely the rug was about to be pulled out from under her at any minute, just as it'd been with her parents and her finances and the magazine.

"But," he said, "I would ask that we didn't go too far to a city. I'd want to stay near my dad and Rosemary."

Of course he would. "You'd compromise that much?"

"I'd change however I needed to change for you, Donna."

She focused on the ground, her vision wet and blurry. She longed to rest her hands on her belly, just as she had caught herself doing so many times lately, the gesture so comfortable.

*Did you hear that?* she thought to their baby. *He'll already do anything for you.*

And she would, too.

When Donna looked up at Caleb again, he seemed as if all he wanted to do was come down off his porch to embrace her, to end all her worries with one all-consuming hug. Her heart sang.

"Caleb," she managed to say. "I'd never want you to change."

He straightened up from the pole, as if she'd said words that had altered his world. That had made his dreams come true.

*Should* she tell him?

Caution—deep-seated, hard-to-shake—got her tongue.

Just as she was wondering what should come next— God, why couldn't she just bring herself to *tell* him?— she heard a sound in her dress pocket.

Her phone.

At first she didn't do anything, but then Caleb laughed, as if thinking, *Isn't that always the way with us?* Then he motioned toward the sound, telling her to just answer it.

When she glanced at the screen, she saw Savannah's number.

## *Chapter Eleven*

That night, the living room of the main house was silent as the Byrds, minus William and Sam, waited on their chairs, poised for the sound of a car to drive up out front.

Donna sat between Tammy and Jenna on the leather sofa. They were fairly composed in comparison to Nathan, whose dark hair was ruffled from running his fingers through it a thousand times. He was standing by the stone fireplace, opening and closing a lighter he occasionally used to smoke cigars outside.

*Click, clack—*

Aidan lingered next to him, and he stared a hole through his younger brother.

"Stop that."

Nathan stilled himself, but only for a minute. Then he was back to it.

*Click, clack—*

"Stop it!" said Donna, Tammy, Jenna and Aidan at the same time.

If the sound hadn't been mocking the stilted rhythm of Donna's heartbeat, she wouldn't have minded so much, but her nerves were fried after talking with Caleb and then having to leave him so abruptly after her phone had rung.

"You should answer it," he'd said when she'd revealed who was on the other end of the line.

She'd told herself that there would be another opportunity for a conversation with him, so she'd picked up Savannah's call....

A wash of illumination swept over the room as a car's headlights beamed through the front window, and Donna came to attention.

Tammy stood and straightened the pretty dress she'd put on. "That's gotta be them."

Donna and Jenna got up from the sofa, too. When Savannah had told Donna on the phone that she and James were in town tonight, staying at Buckshot Hills's only motel and asking if they could meet, there hadn't been much time to prepare anything like hors d'oeuvres or even their nerves.

The doorbell rang, and Tammy rushed to the foyer to get it. Donna felt detached from reality, as if she were watching things happen through a lens.

*Surreal,* she thought. And it got even more so after Donna heard the door opening, voices, then the door shutting.

The next moment, Tammy was leading a woman with straight, chin-edged light blond hair into the room. Her eyes were a deep brown, her face flushed, her figure tiny and trim in the blue lacy blouse, white pants and wedge sandals she was wearing. She appeared at least a decade younger than what Donna knew her age to be.

The notorious Savannah, Donna thought as the woman looked them all over, smiling politely, although tensely.

But the man who followed her into the living room was the person who really drew every gaze.

James Bowie Jeffries was tall and lanky, yet muscled, in his khaki pants, untucked white shirt and Doc Martens boots. He had a mixture of William's and Sam's hair—a thatch of brown highlighted by the sun—and bright blue Byrd eyes.

The spitting image of *both* Uncle William and Dad.

And he was only about a year older than Donna, living proof that Dad had loved someone else before he had supposedly loved Mom. Donna's emotions got even more muddied than usual, although she was trying very hard to be open-minded.

As Tammy came back to the sofa, everyone greeted the new arrivals.

Donna sat again, then said, "Thank you so much for coming."

Nathan, the natural host, motioned to a couple of cherrywood upholstered seats by the fireplace.

Savannah took one of them. "I apologize for not calling earlier than I did."

Her voice was sweet, like honey-laced milk, and Donna could imagine why two young men might've found it appealing, especially with the girl-next-door face that went with it.

She added, "While we drove to Buckshot Hills, I wasn't sure if we'd be turning the car around at some point, and I didn't want to disappoint you if that happened."

She didn't have to explain that their trip had been touch-and-go, filled with doubts about what they were doing. That's probably why Savannah had asked to come over right away tonight—before she or James changed their minds.

James had stayed standing this entire time, and it was telling that he'd distanced himself from Savannah's chair. "What my mom isn't saying is that I've been difficult."

Jenna spoke. "That's understandable."

Leaning against the opposite end of the fireplace from anyone else, James went quiet, merely surveying everyone in the room. He had the air of a man who'd come here only because it was something that needed to get done—and the sooner it was done, the better.

Savannah seemed willing to make up for him. "We're happy we made it."

A fraught moment passed before Donna introduced herself, then went around the room, naming each name.

"Donna," Savannah said, tilting her head and smiling at her. "I'm sorry about all the phone tag we were playing. James was at his home in New Orleans, knee-deep in a project. He becomes a hermit when he's got a deadline."

Donna doubted that was the reason for the holdup, but she would've been just as cautious as James.

Nathan clearly saw an opening for some small talk to lighten the moment. "What do you do for a living, James?"

Savannah answered for him, maybe because she knew

her son wasn't up to trivial chatter. "He's made a quiet fortune with software and computer apps."

James wore an edgy smile. "God knows where I got an aptitude for technology."

His pointed comment about not knowing who his father was sliced down the middle of the room.

This man was hurting, Donna thought. More than any of them, and she couldn't blame him.

She got angry, too—at Sam again, and at Savannah. James could be her brother or at least her cousin. She wanted to know everything about him, but it didn't look like that was going to happen with the way things were going.

Savannah tried to cover the awkwardness by smiling again. Dammit, she was likable, unassuming, but still with a steel magnolia sense about her. It was so hard for Donna to despise her because of what she'd inadvertently done to her parents' marriage and to James.

He seemed restless. "Where're the others?"

He meant William and Sam, and everyone in the room knew it, based on the way they all shifted.

Aidan spoke up. "My dad and uncle will be here shortly."

Donna added, "They wanted us to get to know you first. I hope you don't mind."

"I don't," Savannah said. "It was probably a good idea, seeing as things might get heated."

She sent a glance to James. After Aidan's answer, he had fixed his gaze on the room's entrance, as if he was waiting to face down the two men.

Savannah let out an exasperated sound. "Well, there's not much point in beating around the bush, is there? You kids have questions. Just as many as we do about you, I imagine."

James pulled his gaze from the entrance and wandered over to the front window, leaning against the wall, staring outside. His mouth was firm, as if he were barring himself from everything.

Savannah rested her hands in her lap. "I'm going to tear the bandage from the wound and start things off. Your P.I. might've told you the basics about me, but he couldn't fill in why I did what I did…why I made the decisions I made. I came here to set the record straight, among other matters. I promised James I would."

She glanced at her son, who'd closed his eyes, then opened them again, his gaze still trained out the window.

She waited a moment, as if hoping James would look her way, but he didn't.

Then, with reserved dignity, Savannah started.

"I didn't have a good family life when I was younger. But I had ambition—a hunger to make something of myself and get out of my foster home. I made it all the way to college on scholarship, and I was on track for a much better life."

Donna looked at Jenna. Savannah sounded a lot like them—focused, driven.

Savannah went on. "I always had my nose in my books, until the day William asked me out. Handsome, Prince Charming William. He had everything—good grades, a good family. I respected him and loved being around him. We had a deep affection for each other, and when he started hinting that he wanted me to meet his dad, well…my dream machine took off. It all sounded perfect to me."

"Then," James said, "William had that car accident."

His tone wasn't sarcastic, as Donna had anticipated it might be. It was almost as if listening to his mom handling this with such grace had made him want to support her, even a little.

She gave him a loving, yet somewhat injured glance, then nodded. "William was banged up, with a broken leg being the worst of it all. But school was nearly out for the summer, and I told him I would drive him back to the Flying B and stay with him to nurse him back to health. I didn't tell William that I had nowhere else to go that summer, but I meant what I said. I wanted to be with him. And I wanted to meet the family."

This time, Donna supplied what came next. "My dad was back here for summer vacation, too."

James's gaze connected with hers, and she sent him a sympathetic smile. *I get it—the anger, the isolation. You're not alone.*

She wasn't sure what he was thinking, because he canted back his head and rested it against the wall, listening.

"I'm going to be absolutely truthful," Savannah said, "and I hope I don't hurt any feelings more than they've been hurt. But I owe everyone honesty."

Tammy had been on the edge of the sofa the whole time. "Don't worry about us. Go on."

From across the room, Aidan and Nathan didn't look as sure as their sister. They had their thick arms crossed over their chests.

"When I met Sam…" Savannah said, a faraway look in her eyes now. "How can I say it except, *'Bam'*? It was more powerful than anything I'd ever felt before. And he felt it, too."

Tammy's posture wilted, as if she was feeling sorry for her dad. Nathan's and Aidan's jaws tightened.

"The summer went on," Savannah said, "and Sam and I were more and more drawn to each other. William couldn't get around much with his broken leg, so Sam took to entertaining me. That's where Tex comes in. It was pretty obvious that he favored William over Sam, and there were some competitive issues between the brothers, but Tex seemed happy that they'd been getting along during the summer. I think he was even optimistic that they were going to forge a new kind of relationship."

*So much for that,* Donna thought, dreading what was coming next. She put her arm around Tammy, who leaned into her.

"Tex had put me up in one of the cabins," Savannah said.

*The dream cabin,* Donna thought.

"I think," Savannah added with a slight smile, "he didn't want any funny business going on with me sneaking into William's room in the main house. But that backfired, because, one night after dinner, when I was returning to my cabin, I met Sam along the way. One thing led to another, and…"

She stopped there, appearing remorseful, but also a little wistful. "Sam told me he loved me, and I'd fallen for him, as well. I never wanted to hurt William, and since he was still under the weather, we decided to wait until he got better to tell him about us. I thought about leaving the ranch, too, but again, there was nowhere for me to go. And, truthfully, I couldn't tear myself away from Sam. We just had to find the best way to let William down easy."

By this time, Aidan had walked away from his spot

at the fireplace, clearly having a hard time hearing this. Nathan and Tammy didn't move.

It was Jenna who spoke next. "Dad felt guilty about being with you. He told me."

Savannah smiled gently. "And he told me that he'd never been so in love with anyone before. He didn't think he ever would be again."

Donna thought about how Dad still seemed to have feelings for Savannah, even now. He hadn't lied to Donna about that—only to the wife he'd married on the rebound.

Aidan finally asked a question, his voice wire-tight. "Not long afterward, you and my uncle were caught red-handed."

"Yes," Savannah said. "We were. Tex saw Sam leaving my cabin late one night. He gave Sam hell, and their fight was so ugly that Sam took off in his truck."

Jenna said, "I'm positive he meant to come back, after he cooled off."

"He didn't have the chance," Savannah said. "Tex knocked at my cabin door, then called me every name I deserved—a trollop, a whore. And I couldn't disagree. I was more ashamed than I'd ever been in my life, so I didn't wait for Sam. I talked one of the hands into giving me a ride into town. I left, just as I should've done at the beginning of the summer, when I first saw Sam. Then, about a day later, I heard from a friend that William and Tex and Sam had all gone their separate ways, so I cut ties with Texas A&M and everyone else and decided I would do everything I could to erase myself from the Byrds' lives. Maybe then they could find their ways back to each other, without me standing in between them."

A stinging laugh came from James's corner of the

room. "Because you knew there was an even bigger reason they would all fight with each other."

Savannah looked at him again, her eyes shining with tears. "James is referring to the fact that I was pregnant."

*The grocery receipt,* Donna thought. It was all coming full circle.

"Still," Savannah said, "I decided that no matter who the father was, I was blessed, even though I was still never going back to this ranch."

Donna brushed her hand over her belly. Blessed was right. She felt for Savannah, saw herself in her in a lot of ways.

But the more Savannah spoke, the more Donna began to believe in the rightness of telling Caleb about their child as soon as possible. Just look at what Savannah's secrets had done to this family.

Savannah said, "I came upon a small town in West Texas where I could disappear, fell into a reception job with a woman who decorated homes, and she took me under her wing. Then I had James, and I couldn't have lived a fuller life. My mentor left her business to me—she didn't have any sons or daughters—and then I met a man who married me later in life, after James had gone to college. Years later, after my husband passed away, I got a call from a private investigator, telling me that the Byrd family was looking for me."

"And looking for your son," Donna said, not wanting James to be excluded. "We wanted to get to know him, too."

He glanced at the group, and Donna could see that he was still struggling with his bottled emotions. A man who'd grown up without siblings, a man who'd been a boy without a father.

He had a lot to get used to…if he didn't turn them away.

Tammy asked, "Why didn't you ever contact my dad or Uncle Sam after years had gone by and things had cooled off?"

"There was no way I was going to cause more of a rift than I already had, and I knew this kind of news would stir up old trouble." Savannah's steel was showing now. "And I told Donna already that I'm content to never talk about who the father is. It's up to James to ask, and no one else."

"And I'm not going to," James said.

All of them started to talk, but before there could be any argument, James moved away from the window, silencing everyone.

"I didn't come here to cause a family implosion," he said. "And even if Mom and I have been over a rough road lately, I'm with her on this. From what your P.I. said, it sounds like this family is finally on the mend, and I'll be damned if I'm responsible for messing it up again. No man should be asked to live with that stain on him."

A new voice echoed through the room. "It wouldn't be a stain, James."

Donna whipped around to find both her father and Uncle William at the entrance, where they'd obviously been listening. William's gaze was on Savannah, as if he were seeing a ghost. So was Sam's, but Donna had to look away from him, because it was as if his entire soul was drawn to Savannah.

As if she'd torn it out when she'd left.

Savannah, herself, was wearing a poker face as she gripped her armrests.

God, Donna wanted to leave the room, leave them all alone to work this out. Uncle William looked conflicted about Savannah, and maybe even James, whom he now watched as if he was seeing a second spirit, one who resembled both him and his brother. Tammy had once told Donna that Uncle William, a widower and very much settled in his bachelorhood, wasn't sure how to react to the news of a possible love child, and here was proof.

But Dad... As he turned his gaze to James, he paled, fisting his hands by his sides.

James merely stood ramrod straight again by the window, his expression more embattled than ever.

Jenna was pulling at Donna's hand. *Time for privacy. Time to let William, Savannah, James and Dad talk this out.*

As everyone but the main players headed from the room, toward the patio, Jenna held on to Donna's hand, keeping her back from the group as the rest of them went outside.

"That was something," Jenna said.

Her voice was shaking, and Donna hugged her close.

Jenna whispered, "You think Dad'll be okay?"

"I think," Donna said, as they pulled away from each other, "we need to be his daughters more than ever, after the debris clears."

And as she thought of James inside that living room, a casualty of secrets, she put a hand to her belly, knowing that she needed to go to Caleb tonight.

Caleb had been bound and determined not to fall asleep.

He knew tonight was make-or-break on a lot of levels—with the Byrds, and with him and Donna.

If she needed him at all, it would be after the emotional fallout that was sure to come with Savannah's visit. So he'd showered, put on a pair of sweats and a T-shirt, then planted himself on a lounger in front of a show about cops in the bayou.

But the long day got to him, and he floated off, dreaming of blond hair, blue eyes and that kiss Donna had initiated before he'd left the ranch a few weeks ago.

A rapping at his door yanked him out of his light slumber, and he clicked off the TV, combing the hair back from his face with his fingers. When he opened the door, he found Donna standing in the lantern light.

"I know it's late," she said.

"It's never too late." He opened the door all the way, his pulse on fire, warming him.

She'd come back, just as if she did need him.

Once inside, she surveyed his cabin with its rodeo paintings and plaid curtains. He realized that this was the first time she'd been inside his home.

When she sat in a chair, he thought she was finally right where she belonged—with him. But when her body seemed to lose everything that had been keeping her together and she buried her face in her hands, Caleb wasn't so sure.

He went to her, bending to a knee, putting a hand on her back. "Want to talk about it?"

"They're gone now."

"Savannah and James."

"Yes. When they left, they said goodbye to us, and Tammy had the presence of mind to invite them to dinner tomorrow."

"So it went well?"

Donna raised her face from her hands, her gaze so tired that he ached to gather her into his arms and tell her everything would turn out fine.

"There were no nuclear explosions," Donna said. "At least, not before Uncle William and Dad came into the room. But after Savannah and James left, Dad told Jenna and me that their private conversation started off badly. James is carrying a grudge, and he really let Dad have it. He doesn't blame William for anything, though."

"Didn't both of them sleep with her?"

Donna nodded, then told him the entire story Savannah had related. Caleb had known some of it, and he could see why James would've seen Sam as the bad guy.

"James had already let his mom know how he feels about her part in it," Donna said, rubbing her temples. "So it was Dad's turn tonight."

"James got it out of his system. That's a good thing."

"I'm not sure. He's carrying a lot around with him. It's obvious from the way he cuts himself off from everyone. He could be my brother, but I'm not certain he's the type of man you can ever know."

Caleb stroked her hair back from her face. "That's what I would've said about you, once upon a time."

Her eyes went teary.

"Hey, now," he said. "I wasn't being cruel."

"I know you weren't."

After a moment, she told him the rest of it. Then added, "I think the problems are only beginning. When all of us left Savannah and James alone with our dads, we met in the backyard. We started to debate about whether we should try to persuade James to ask for a paternity test."

"It's no one's place to do that."

"I agree. But the arguments aren't going to end there. From the way our dads were carrying themselves at the end of the night, it looked like there was a wall between them again. They were always naturally competitive, and actually seeing James might've given new life to that."

"It was a charged night, Donna. Things'll calm down."

"But, already, it's as if it's Byrd against Byrd again."

All Caleb could do was keep stroking her hair.

He knew in his heart that, even though he'd never had a long-term girlfriend or a wife, this was how it should be between two people: supporting each other. Honest in everything. Helping each other through thick and thin.

She slid her hand into his, and there was a new fear in her eyes. He wasn't sure why.

"Tonight," she said, her voice wavering, "I found out from Savannah that she left the ranch and never contacted Dad or William again because she didn't want to force them into a decision that might throw their lives into chaos. But look at what her silence did." She shook her head. "Look at what keeping secrets *does*."

As she searched his gaze with her own, he got a bad feeling in the pit of his stomach.

She took a shaky breath. "I might be too emotional right now, but I saw how Savannah's decisions hurt James, and I…"

When she touched her belly, Caleb let go of her hand. Instinctual, a moment of suspicious shock.

What was she saying?

"Caleb," she said through tears now. "I'm going to have a baby."

It was as if a giant hammer had come down from the roof, swinging into him and knocking him over. The news reverberated through him, his thoughts ringing.

Hadn't they used a condom?

Had there been a leak?

He thought of how he hadn't really checked it after they'd made love, because Donna had been touching him, gearing him up for another go and his mind hadn't been in smart mode.

"A...baby?" he asked dumbly.

But an instant after he uttered it, he was already smiling. He couldn't imagine what he would want more than a child who had Donna's eyes and her brains and...well, her everything.

He'd spent a lifetime sowing his wild oats, but he was ready now.

He was so happy, it took him a second or two to recognize the shadows in Donna's gaze, and with a falling sensation, he knew intuitively that they weren't there because she was having a baby.

They were there because she was having a baby with *him*.

Suddenly, every excuse she had used to put him off swatted at him: she was a city girl and he was a country boy. She went to fancy restaurants and he wore suits from the depths of his closet and served skillet steaks.

She still thought she was too good for him and she was trapped by a pregnancy.

His chest seemed to crack open. Here was the truth—one that was on naked display in front of him.

"You're never going to change your mind about me, are you?" he asked.

Now her tears clouded his view of her eyes, and he wasn't sure if he'd seen those shadows or not.

"I already have changed my mind, Caleb."

She got out of the chair and, as he took a step away from her rather than toward her this time, she paused.

"Caleb?"

He held up a hand, numb. The truth did that to a person, made them numb. It also gave them time to allow pain in.

*Could you be more useless?* his dad had once said to him, not long ago. And then there'd been the recent, *Useless idiot.*

Donna thought the same about him, didn't she? He was pretty sure he'd seen it in her very gaze tonight.

"I've been pursuing you for over a month, all the time believing in fate," he said. "I didn't even need to have any dream on that mattress to tell me what I wanted out of life."

When she got a guilty look on her face, his heart split even more.

"*Did* you have a dream?"

She hung her head, nodding, but then she looked up again. "I was in a field, laughing, touching my stomach. It was a good dream, Caleb, but I wasn't sure how I felt about you, so I didn't say anything."

"Because you're never going to be sure." He cut out a laugh. "I should've seen it long before now. Maybe I'm as idiotic as my dad says."

"*Don't* say that." She was pointing at him, her tone furious. "I know you don't believe that."

Did he? He wasn't sure, especially now. When the woman you thought you loved had those kind of thoughts about you, you couldn't be sure about anything.

"You couldn't hide what you really feel just now, as you told me about the baby," Caleb said. "That one moment—that flash into your soul—I could see it in your eyes, Donna. You don't want me to be the father."

She was moving toward him again, but he put up his hand once more.

"I wasn't sure at first," she said thickly. "I won't lie to you about that, but—"

He turned on his heel, unable to hear anymore. On his way to the door, he grabbed his keys from an unused ashtray, then went for his boots, pulling them on.

"I would never force you into living with a man you can't respect, Donna. We'll work something out with our baby, but I won't live the rest of my life knowing that, deep inside, you think you just settled for me. That you had no choice in being with me because we shared one night together and it didn't mean a damned thing to you in the end."

"But it did."

He blocked her out as he pulled open the door, but she put her hand against it, closing it.

His voice didn't sound like his own. "Don't even pretend anymore."

"I'm not pretending."

He almost stayed…and he would've if she had said what he needed most to hear.

That she had fallen for him, too.

The optimist inside him whispered, *She's coming around to it. Just give her a little more time.*

But he'd already waited too long, and look what it'd gotten him—a destroyed heart.

"Unfortunately," he said, "I don't believe you'll ever change enough to stop pretending with me."

Cleary crushed, she backed away, and he told himself to go forward, out the door, don't look back.

And he didn't look back—not even after he started his truck's engine and drove away, unsure of where to go.

Or what he'd just done.

## Chapter Twelve

"Donna?"

It was the next day, and Donna had just needed to get away, licking yet one more set of wounds.

So when she heard Jenna's voice outside the dream cabin door, she didn't answer. Anguish kept pummeling her as she lay on the dream mattress, the ceiling as blank as she felt. She'd come here to see if she would dream of the future once more, but there'd been nothing, only the sound of her heart murmuring his name again and again.

Caleb. She'd never known that she could miss anyone so much, even though he was still on the same ranch, a few minutes away. But it felt like a million miles. Worse yet, the distance seemed too far to ever cross, no matter how long she walked; it would keep stretching and stretching, rolling beneath her like the treadmill it felt as if she'd been on for months now.

"Donna," Jenna said again, "please open the door for me and Tammy. You're starting to worry us."

She closed her eyes, hugging her arms over her belly. There was one good thing that had come out of this at least. Her baby. All day, she'd been thinking of names, but then she would get sidetracked yet again.

What would Caleb think of *Emma?* Or *Kyle?* Or…

The sound of the lock being tampered with brought Donna out of the bed, and she went to the door, opening it.

Both Jenna and Tammy were waiting, Jenna holding a key. Their eyes were wide with concern.

"What's wrong?" Jenna asked.

A year ago, the city girl in Donna would've laughed, shrugged and moved on from a bad night.

But not the woman who'd gone through an ego-breaking financial crisis and now this ultimate heartache.

Grief finally overtook her, and she bit her lip to keep herself from crying. Not that it did any good, because the tears came anyway.

Tammy and Jenna came to the rescue, entering the cabin to embrace her.

That just made the tears come harder. "Caleb…" she said, barely getting his name out.

Jenna guided her farther into the room, to the bed. They sat down while Tammy closed the door.

"What about Caleb?" Jenna asked.

"I told him about the baby."

Tammy leaned back against the door, her eyes even wider now. Donna had almost forgotten that she'd told only Jenna about the pregnancy.

And Caleb.

Her crying began anew as Jenna comforted her. She cried every tear she'd held back all these years and, eventually, she was too tired to continue.

As Jenna brushed the water off Donna's face, she softly said, "We all need a good cry every once in a while, especially after... What *did* happen with Caleb after you told him about the baby?"

"He looked happy." Donna swiped at her face. Damned stray tears.

"Happy is good, isn't it?"

Donna shook her head. "It didn't last long, because he saw the look I must've had on my face. All my doubts were there, and he saw them. It was the last straw for him, I think. He said we would work something out with the baby because he'd been wasting his time with me."

"He said that?" Tammy asked.

"Basically." When Donna sniffed, Jenna got up to fetch her a tissue. "I crossed a line, and I don't know if he'll let me back over it. I didn't mean for it to turn out this way...."

The room was quiet for a second, but then Tammy said, "Hugh will swear that Caleb's a stand-up guy, Donna. Same with the rest of the hands. He won't let you down."

"No, you should've seen him," Donna said. "He was crushed, and I'm pretty sure it was because my doubts validated everything he's heard from his dad."

"Like what?" Jenna asked.

"That he's useless, without value. His dad says things like that because of his dementia, but they're far from true." A wobble of emotion threatened to take her down again. "Caleb told me that I hadn't changed enough for him to believe that I want him. That hurt a lot."

Jenna sat next to her on the bed again. "If you could see how you've changed from then until now, you might not recognize yourself. Do you realize how far you've come since we moved to this ranch and since you started seeing Caleb?"

An answer stuck in Donna's throat. Yes, she *thought* she'd noticed a change in herself. That's why Caleb's words last night had wounded her so thoroughly.

*I don't believe you'll ever change enough to stop pretending with me.*

"Do you think," she asked in a raw voice, "Caleb will ever believe that I want to be with him? That I…"

Fell in love with him?

As Donna gathered herself, she knew this was true. Love had happened somewhere along the line. Maybe not at first sight, but it had come slowly, as he had patiently courted her.

But did she have any shot of convincing Caleb of how she felt?

And how could she do it?

Jenna and Tammy were still waiting for Donna to complete her last sentence.

She sat straighter on the bed. "I fell in love with him. I really did."

Both women smiled, as if Donna had taken forever to come to a conclusion that had been obvious from the get-go.

Jenna took Donna by the hand, helping her off the bed. "Come to the house with us. Savannah and James aren't here yet for dinner, but they should be soon."

Tammy said, "After they leave, we can talk more about Caleb. Plan a little."

"Get him right back where you should be with him," Jenna said.

Donna felt better already. Then, with one last hug, they all went out the door, walking to the main house. Once there, Donna went to her room to freshen up.

By the time she got downstairs, her mind was exploding with questions.

How should she go forward with Caleb? How should she even approach him? And would he give her the opportunity to spill her heart out to him, the right way this time?

She went out back so she could collect her thoughts before dinner, sitting in a chair by the splashing fountain. Every play of water reminded her of the night Caleb had come out here to try to kiss her.

She rested her hand on her tummy, rubbing it. *We're going to figure this out. Don't worry.*

Then she heard footsteps, and she sat up, her heart thudding.

But it wasn't Caleb who stood nearby—it was James, who had wandered outside with a cocktail glass in hand, watching Donna as if he hadn't expected to find anyone else out here. Under the surrendering sun, his blond-brown hair looked burnished, his lean form shadowed by the bucking bronco fountain sculpture.

"Sorry," he said. "I didn't mean to impose. I thought I'd find myself alone."

He looked so much like Uncle William and Sam—her father—right now, especially her father, and in more than just the superficial blue-eyed way. James and Dad were both carrying the same frustrated tautness and the same haunting darkness in their gazes.

The resemblance kicked something into motion inside Donna, and she started talking, just as honestly as she should've been talking to Caleb or her sister or Dad or anyone else, all along.

"We really don't know each other, James," she said. "And I firmly believe that any decisions you make about this family or discovering the identity of your father are none of my business, but I'm going to say this, anyway."

He seemed to gird himself, yet she was too far gone to stop.

"I'm a lot like Savannah. I had a secret, too, and what I mean by that is… Well, I'm having a baby—the same secret she carried. And I mishandled the way the father discovered the news, just like your mom did."

James's spine had gone stiff, as it'd been last night when they'd first met. "You don't need to tell me any of this, Donna."

"Yes, I do, because if I can do anything to put *my* new family together as well as *our* new family, there shouldn't be anything that stops us."

James assessed her with those Byrd-blue eyes. Was he going to tell her to go to hell? That this definitely wasn't her business?

But then his gaze strayed to her belly, which she was touching again.

"A baby, huh?" he said.

She nodded.

"Congratulations." He furrowed his brow. "I guess that's going to make me either an uncle or…"

Donna smiled, too. "Wouldn't you like to know for certain what you'll be to this child? I mean, either way I hope you'll be an important part of his or her life, but wouldn't it be nice to know if I'm carrying your niece or nephew?"

"Or a second cousin." James smiled for the first time she could recall. "I'd like to be an uncle someday, though. I don't ever plan on having kids, but I'd be a great uncle. One of those cool ones who plays with computers too much and sneaks the kids treats."

"I'd like that, too. Very much."

Just as she wondered if James was about to decide that he wanted a paternity test, he paused. She had no idea what might've been going on in his head, but then again, he didn't give her a lot of time to analyze, because he toasted her with his drink, then sauntered back toward the house.

Nonetheless, Donna's heart warmed as she glanced off into the distance, in the direction Caleb's cabin was located.

As the sun set, the space between her and that cabin felt shorter than it ever had, and she scooted to the edge of her seat.

It was time to cover the distance that separated them.

Caleb shouldn't have taken the day off, but he'd done it, anyway.

He felt like crap for what he'd said to Donna last night, and he wished that he could be with her now as the sun dipped below the horizon. He wished that he could put his head to her stomach, getting close to their child.

And he wished that he hadn't said a lot of things that just weren't true.

First, he shouldn't have told Donna that she would never change from who she'd been, because that had only come out in a defensive way. But he also shouldn't have said that he might be just as idiotic as his dad told him he was.

Sure, he'd thought that the sentiment had been written all over Donna's face when she'd told him about the baby, but was it the truth?

The more he thought about it, the more he believed her when she'd told him he was wrong. Still, the little boy in him who'd heard "useless idiot" from his dad couldn't help but to put stock in those words.

Maybe Caleb had taken the day off and come here to tell Dad that he was wrong, and he could be *very* useful, as a son…and as a father and husband. Or maybe Caleb needed to convince himself more than anyone.

Dad had been napping when Caleb arrived, and that, plus Caleb's presence, had allowed Aunt Rosemary to leave the house to go to the tearoom in town. He hadn't mentioned anything about Donna or the baby to her. He even hid his troubles under the smile he always reserved for Rosemary, who didn't need any more discord introduced into her life.

After she'd left, Caleb had sat down in front of the TV, not really seeing what was on it.

A couple of hours must've passed, because Dad eventually meandered out of his room. Caleb looked for signs in his dad about what kind of day it would be.

Dad was quiet, so it was hard to tell. Caleb got him a snack—a bran muffin and orange juice—then took to the couch as Dad channel surfed.

When he settled on a woman's fashion show, Caleb knew something was up, and he turned to his father.

He was watching him. Shock jolted Caleb, because it was the first time in a long time that he could see his dad in those eyes. They seemed clear. Lucid.

Or was he wrong?

"What's got you down?" Dad asked.

Emotion crumpled up in Caleb's throat, but he swallowed it away. "Nothing. I'm doing fine."

Dad just kept looking at him, and Caleb didn't know what to say or think.

Finally, Dad rested his head against the back of his chair, closing his eyes. "A solid man is a man who's always around for a loved one."

And he went silent, breathing evenly.

At his dad's cryptic comment, the jagged ball in Caleb's throat returned. Had Dad been insinuating that he *wasn't* a solid man because Dad didn't remember everything Caleb had done for him and he didn't know how often he'd been around? Or had he known that this was his son he'd been addressing? Had he even been referring to how Caleb had bought this house for his family and was taking care of them now?

Had his dad been thanking him in the best way a distant man could?

As Caleb turned to the TV again, a smile captured him through and through.

He would never be able to be one hundred percent sure, but he was damned well going to take this as a good day.

Rosemary returned before Dad woke up, and Caleb went back to the ranch, a certain weight lifted from his chest.

There was a bigger one that remained, though, and he wanted to stand beneath Donna's window as the day melted away, wanted to send her one of those flippant text messages and bring her to the sill so she could lean over it to talk to him.

But had he turned her off for good last night? Would

she, a modern city woman, say good riddance and leave the ranch with their baby, daring him to challenge her?

Caleb remembered the decimated expression on her face, and he just wasn't sure.

After driving up the road to the ranch, he passed by the main house, every muscle telling him to turn into the driveway. But every doubtful cell inside of him was also warning him to wait, to think carefully about what he should say to Donna.

He would formulate a plan of attack. That was the way to do it. And tonight, he'd...

What?

How should he go about this?

When he drove up to his cabin, his plan of attack crumbled before it even started because right there on his porch sat Donna.

All his anguish fell to the wayside, and he'd barely cut the engine before he got out of the truck, taking a couple steps toward her as she rose from her chair, coming toward him, too.

Without a word, they closed the distance between them, step by step, finally meeting in the middle.

His pulse beat in his ears as he read her expression.

Did he dare hope he saw what he thought he saw?

She embraced him, just as he scooped her up into his arms and held her to him, intending never to let go.

"I was so wrong," she said, the words rushing out of her while Caleb held her up against his body.

She'd knocked off his cowboy hat in her fervor, but it wasn't because she was trying to get them to a bed this time. It was because all she wanted to do was be next to him, body and soul.

"And I shouldn't have left you last night," he said, cupping the back of her head until her cheek was pressed against his.

Then, in a burst of elation, she kissed him, hardly able to believe that he was willing to forgive her.

He hadn't let her down after all.

As he still held her, she pushed his hair back from his face, looking into his eyes.

Those forever blue eyes.

"I meant it when I said I believe in you, Caleb. And that I've changed."

"I know you have. But I was stinging from pride last night. I was wrong about so many things."

"But you're not wrong for me. I love you, Caleb." Her voice was breaking. "I love you so much that I couldn't eat or sleep without you. It's you I want—not the city, and definitely not raising our child alone."

"You won't have to. I'm here, Donna. I'm never going to be anywhere else."

They kissed again and, unlike before, this wasn't about pistoning heartbeats or torn-off clothing or the pursuit of satiation. This was about them, together.

A family of three now.

He carried her up the porch steps and into his cabin, kicking the door closed behind him, sitting her gently down on his bed. He got to his knees, then leaned his head against her belly, just as if he'd been wishing to do this the whole day.

"You won't be able to feel him or her kick for a while," Donna whispered, stroking Caleb's hair.

"It doesn't matter. I know someone's in there."

Someone who had brought two of the most unlikely

people together, Donna thought. The youngest match-maker in history.

It seemed enough for them to hold each other like this, but soon, she reclined on the bed, and he kept his head against her as she played with his hair.

When he kissed her stomach, she automatically rocked against him, because just one kiss from him did that to her.

What would a lifetime of them do?

She threaded her fingers through his hair as he kept nuzzling her belly. A pounding cadence began to throb between her legs.

"I should be having dinner with Savannah and James," she whispered.

"I think they'll understand why you'll be late." He lifted her blouse, pressing his lips to her bare stomach while working at the buttons on his shirt.

She wiggled, biting her lip, then saying, "They're going to be our family now. I'm not going to rest until they both see that we're not letting them go."

"That's my Donna," he said as he pushed her blouse up higher. "Relentless."

And she was powerless, too, as he kissed her some more. She always had been that way with him, even if she'd fought what was between them tooth and nail.

After helping him take off her blouse, she pushed the material off the bed, and he slid up her body.

The sensation of his skin against her breasts sent her reeling—a whispering tumble of water that was turning into a growling rush, moment by moment.

"Will you help me to stay away from the hay on this ranch?" she asked as he got ready to kiss her. "It makes me sneeze."

"So you really do want to stay."

"You're here. My family's here."

He smiled, flashing those dimples. "I'll do anything I need to do for you. Anything else?"

"Can I redecorate this cabin?"

"You can even do that, Donna Byrd."

He explored her mouth with his, parting her lips with his tongue, slowly engaging her in rhythmic pleasure. Meanwhile, Donna reached between them to undo her bra.

"I want to feel you," she said against his mouth. "All of you. It seems like it's been forever."

"Hasn't it been?"

She laughed as he unzipped her jeans, then took off the rest of her clothing, leaving her bared to him.

As he watched, she coasted her fingers over her tummy, wondering when the baby would start to show. With all her heart, she knew Caleb's eyes would fill with even more adoration when he saw her belly grow, that he would love this child as much as she already did.

He was on his knees on the floor again, but now he took her by the hips, pulling her toward him.

A restless sigh escaped Donna, and he grinned that cocky grin she'd longed to see, then worked her legs over his shoulders.

When his mouth kissed her most private place, she let out a cry. And as he loved her, slowly, tenderly, she moved her hips with him, liquid pressure building inside of her.

Simmering.

Bubbling.

Boiling until she couldn't hold back any longer and she called his name, desperate and delirious.

As she came to her peak, he was with her all the way, making her crash, moan, say his name again and again.

Then he undressed, too, going to the bed, pulling her on top of him.

He was already hard, and she straddled his hips, taking him in, then churning on top of him.

*My baby's father,* she thought, watching his face, his pleasure, as he climbed to the same steaming place she had already been.

When he climaxed, he gripped her hips, and she laid herself against his length, skin to skin.

Future husband to future wife.

Donna was so swept away that she couldn't hold back, and she whispered in his ear.

"Marry me, Caleb."

He chuckled, utterly breathless. "Marry *me*."

They laughed, and it felt good to do it together, their bodies still against each other.

He touched her belly, and they both quieted.

"I don't want to wait, Donna," he said. "You'd better marry me before the year's out."

She snuggled her face into his neck and smiled, knowing she'd found exactly where she belonged.

"There's nothing I want more, cowboy."

## Epilogue

*Four Months Later*

Laughter from the crowd at the Flying B and B guest barbecue dinner filled the air from a distance as Donna lay on a blanket, blocked from the party by a few old oak trees.

She looked up at the perfect November blue sky, tucking a hand under her head. Birds warbled from a nearby oak as she laughed along with everyone else.

The B and B's opening months had been more successful than any Byrd could've dreamed, but that wasn't all. Over at the barbecue, the entire family was in attendance because Aidan and Nathan had announced that they had finally gotten a geological survey going on the west side of the ranch, where their undeveloped property given to them by Tex had been waiting.

There was a lot to celebrate, and the Byrds tended

to throw a party for just about everything these days—
Tammy and Mike's wedding, then Jenna and J.D.'s. Soon
there would even be a baby shower for Donna and Caleb's child.

She used her thumb to play with the diamond ring on
her finger, her other hand resting on her rounding belly.
A loose flannel country dress draped her, barely showing how she had just started to pop.

*All I wish,* she thought to her baby, *is that you could've
met your great-grandpa.*

She sighed, closing her eyes and picturing Tex holding his great-grandchild in his arms.

But when she heard footsteps moving through the
grass nearby, she glanced toward the sound.

It was Savannah, and she was smiling down at Donna.

"Mind if I join you?" she asked.

"Please do."

The sun shone on her chin-length blond hair. In the
sunlight, there were faint wisps of silver visible—not
that this made Savannah look any older.

Donna had uncovered some old pictures at Dad's
house a couple months ago, and she and Jenna had painstakingly gone through every one that showed their mom,
who was doing things like cradling the two of them as
they said cheese to the camera in their little-girl dresses.

Donna hadn't realized it at first, but there was something about Savannah that reminded her of Mom. Was
it the light hair? The kind eyes?

But that wasn't the only realization for Donna. Had
Mom reminded Dad of Savannah? Was that why he'd
married her?

Any way about it, Savannah had become a part of
their lives. She had accepted monthly invitations to stay

at the B and B, and James had even visited a time or two himself, hunkering down in one of the cabins to work on his projects. He was still bullheadedly maintaining that he didn't want to know the identity of his father, but some of the Byrds had their fingers crossed.

Savannah turned her face to the sun. "It's good to get away from the crowd for a few minutes."

Donna didn't ask if Savannah needed a break because of Uncle William and Dad. They'd all been on tentative ground since she'd come into their lives and, while William still didn't show his emotional hand around an equally neutral Savannah, Dad sure did. His heart was in his eyes every time he looked at her.

But that's the way the Byrds were, Donna thought. A walking, talking drama that would probably never end, even if they'd come pretty far.

As Donna kept surveying Savannah, the birds sang, the laughter still sounding in the near distance, her hand lingering on the curve of her tummy.

Savannah caught Donna watching her, and she laughed. "What is it?"

Should she ask?

Oh, why not.

"I've been meaning to broach a particular topic with you. The cabin you stayed in so long ago…?"

"I heard that you all call it the dream cabin now."

Donna propped herself up on her elbows. "Then you've heard the stories about the bed."

"I did."

"Did *you* ever have a dream on the mattress?"

Savannah pressed her lips together, and Donna was sure she would never tell. But when the woman glanced at her, Donna saw the same haunted shade in her gaze as she always saw in her father's.

"I did have a dream," she said. "I remember swinging in a swing that hung from one of these old oaks on the property. There were two men in front of me, and even though their backs were turned, I knew who they were."

Donna could make an educated guess on her end. Uncle William and her father, Sam.

"I swung higher and higher," Savannah said. "Then, I couldn't hold on anymore. I went flying through the air, and I was so afraid of crashing to the dirt. But I was exhilarated, too."

"Did you hit the ground and wake up?"

"No." Savannah knit her brows. "One of those men turned around and caught me."

"Who?"

A mysterious smile appeared as she stood, brushing off her crisp tan pants.

"I'll see you at the barbecue, Donna."

As Savannah left, Donna lay back down, watching the sky. Was that mattress an excuse for everyone's psyche to work itself out? Or was it really magic?

More importantly, which man had caught Savannah, and did that mean anything for the future?

She closed her eyes. Maybe they would find out in time, but for now, she listened to those birds, the laughter. And when she felt Caleb's presence, she didn't look over at him.

She knew it was him. She always would.

He settled down next to her on the blanket as she smiled.

"Ready to eat yet?" he asked.

"Soon."

This time, she varied her mattress dream, taking *his* hand and putting it on her belly.

When he kissed her, a memory of the dream she'd had on the night she'd first been with Caleb swirled in Donna's mind. But now it turned into something new: an image of her, Caleb and their child on this same blanket, sitting beneath the sun on the Flying B and laughing with each other.

A dream that was *definitely* in their future.

\* \* \* \* \*

"Do you have a long-range business plan?"

She laughed softly. "I love this place. I'll do anything to keep it."

"There's no sense driving yourself to an early grave over a piece of land, Annie."

"Spoken like a vagabond. Well, I've been a vagabond. Roots are so much better." She shoved away from the railing. "I have work to do."

Annie went inside, her good mood having fizzled. What did he know about the need to own, to succeed? He didn't have a child to support and raise right. Who was he to give such advice?

Mitch hadn't come in by the time Austin went to bed and she'd showered and retreated to her own room. It wasn't even dark yet. She pulled down her shades, blocking the dusky sky. Usually she dropped off almost the instant her head hit the pillow.

Tonight she listened for sounds of him, the stranger she was trusting to treat her and her son right. After a while, she heard him come in, then the click of the front door lock.

A few minutes later the shower came on. She pictured him shampooing his hair, which curled down his neck a little, inviting fingers to twine it gently.

Some time passed after the water turned off. Was he shaving? Yes. She could hear the tap of his razor against the sink edge. If they were a couple, he would be coming to bed clean and smooth shaven….

The bathroom door opened and closed, followed by his bedroom door. After that there was only the quiet of a country night, marked occasionally by an animal rustling beyond her open window. She'd finally stopped jumping at strange noises, had stopped getting up to look out her window, wondering what was there. She could identify most of the sounds now.

And tonight she would sleep even better, knowing a strong man was next door. She could give up her fears for a while, get a solid night's sleep and face the new day not alone, not putting on a show of being okay and in control for Austin.

Now if she could just do something about her suddenly-come-to-life libido, all would be right in her world.

\*\*\*

*Don't miss* **A COWBOY'S RETURN** *by USA TODAY bestselling author Susan Crosby.*

*Available June 2013 from Harlequin® Special Edition® wherever books are sold.*